About the Author

The author, Anna String, lives in Cape Town. Her home is a reflection of herself, and she lives with a mental health condition. She has crafted characters that grapple with life, and that have a spiritual yearning just like herself, always searching for more in life. She hopes that through her storytelling, others might find hope and inspiration.

Niaina: A Spirit Life

Anna String

Niaina: A Spirit Life

Olympia Publishers
London

www.olympiapublishers.com
OLYMPIA PAPERBACK EDITION

Copyright © Anna String 2025

The right of Anna String to be identified as author of
this work has been asserted in accordance with sections 77 and 78 of
the Copyright, Designs and Patents Act 1988.

All Rights Reserved

No reproduction, copy or transmission of this publication
may be made without written permission.
No paragraph of this publication may be reproduced,
copied or transmitted save with the written permission of the publisher,
or in accordance with the provisions
of the Copyright Act 1956 (as amended).

Any person who commits any unauthorised act in relation to
this publication may be liable to criminal
prosecution and civil claims for damage.

A CIP catalogue record for this title is
available from the British Library.

ISBN: 978-1-83543-116-0

This is a work of fiction.
Names, characters, places and incidents originate from the writer's
imagination. Any resemblance to actual persons, living or dead, is
purely coincidental.

First Published in 2025

Olympia Publishers
Tallis House
2 Tallis Street
London
EC4Y 0AB

Printed in Great Britain

Part 1

How to not make children, a guide

Hayley, a neuro-diverse person with a zest for life, shares her journey of how to not make children. In this short story, she discusses social ills, such as racism and inequality, and what might be wrong with the world. Through her experiences with different men, she has brushes with alcoholism, intimate partner violence, and even an accidental rape. She encounters people on the brink of despair, reaching out for a bit of humanity. She considers the adoption route, a sperm donor, and whether or not to become a single mum. In spite of being waylaid several times, she at last reconnects with and rediscovers her true love. And finds that sometimes, different ways of thinking and seeing the world can be overcome. Join her in this epic adventure of a life well lived in South Africa. And learn about the essence of a woman who grappled with her fertility and life purpose.

Chapter 1

1. The Queen Bee (me) (Hayley)
And finding myself

My name is Hayley. I believe we have been introduced. If we haven't met yet, know this about me. I am a student of psychology. A learner of things. A girl who likes to write. A mad person. A slightly off-the-wall individual. I am kooky at best, insane at worst. I live with a chronic condition called schizoaffective disorder. It means that I think too much. I overthink, and I go into overdrive. Similar to bipolar, yet different. Not as manic, yet sometimes depressed. Most days, I am fine. Almost normal. Others, I want to scream down the world. Because it's a strange place. And this strangeness sometimes bothers me to the nth degree.

And yet I am the queen bee. Without me, the hive does not function. It doesn't even exist. I let the bees move in to my garden recently. Wild honey bees. They are comfortable here. They have found a home. They are my new friends. So are the slugs, the snails, the praying mantis, the snakes, the squirrels, the birds, the pigeons, the cats and all the other animals here. Occasionally, humans. They, too, are my friends, but for other reasons. I love them at times and fear for them at other times. Which leads me back to the strangeness of the world.

Something is wrong. And I am about to find out what that is. This time, it's not me. It's not even about me.

I have spent a long time in search of myself. And I have

found myself. Through my life so far, my ancestors, my family and relatives, my friends and colleagues, and through strangers, and myself. Not just through relationships with others but also simply in myself. My essence has been revealed to me. The inner workings of my brain have been unravelled and presented to me. My character exposed. My true purpose brought home to me. And this I will share throughout.

So, what is it that is wrong? I am mapping together the pieces of a puzzle. It is to do with the shape of the world. Almost like piecing back together a broken brain. Mending it takes time. In some eastern cultures, if you break a vase, you do not throw it away. You keep the pieces and put them back together with a special glue. You let the former cracks show. As this is what now holds the shape together. This is an ancient art. The lines of the glue become its new beauty.

And so it is with the world today. However, we decide to repair it, the cracks will show. They will form the new essence. And hold things together.

But what is it that is broken?

It is that there is an ongoing rape of the earth. And of its people. There are wars, there is famine, there is inequality, and there is poverty. There are many social ills; there is racism and sexism; there are conflicts, and there is pain. The earth, its people, its wildlife and nature are suffering. And we are the only ones who can change, challenge that and reverse this course. It is time now.

No more.

As I delve deeper into the abyss, I discover that there are others. Who are open-minded, who can see. Who have heard, and who know the way. So, it is with great hope in my heart that I can tell you, we are not alone. There are many guides. Although be aware of false prophets. But look for the light within. And you will always be guided. For this power lies in you, me and all of us, to reach beyond, clutch at the stars. And to find a path to a world that is heaven on earth.

The greatest enemy is those who are driven by their fears. Those who are not free. Those who suffered seek vengeance. Those who indulge in hate and intolerance. Those who accept the bad and let it settle. Those who become pedantic, dogmatic and power-hungry. Those who refuse to love and stop others from speaking and living their truth. The closed-minded and those dripping in a slick of black sludge. Dark matter is upon some, and they need to be liberated of this. The dark can be diffused. It can be disintegrated and destroyed.

Only with love and with light.

It did take a long time for me to find myself. The question is whether I am brave enough to make myself visible. I once cursed my enemies. I said they would never know me, hear me, see me, meet me, find me, or have anything to do with me. That was their punishment. To emerge in a world that is even darker than it was before is a challenge. But I will meet that challenge. I can emerge. As me myself and I, my true self, my original self, unfiltered and untamed. Wild and free, hopeful and imaginative, diplomatic and communicative as I am. Hidden I no longer need to be. For my enemies will fade away. And who will remain are the ones I need to speak with, connect to, work with and live together with.

So, what am I? And why me?

I am a girl who has made a home. A girl who has waited for a man for fifteen years. I am a person who loves. Beyond that, I am also just a being. A being on a spiritual level. A human. One who seeks to connect, to learn and love? I have a deep interest in psychology, the mind, and its capabilities: a keen sense of discovery; a strong love for all things food-related; a bond with my home and my garden of Eden; a need to nurture and mentor others, those younger than myself, and a desire to map the stars.

It's me because my mother was verified by the original beekeeper and her stone mason husband with a simple gift of a lifelong friendship and a giant beeswax candle. I inherited that power from her. The candle still sits on her mantlepiece above the fireplace, which is scattered with an arrangement of ducks, figures, combs, and many special items. The views let us see across the valley. My mother's house is important too. But I have established my own, and it even has a name.

It is the house of Niaina.

Niaina is translated as the place of no one and nowhere. It is my home. Hayley's house. It defines me, and I define it. It has windows and French doors that lead out into the garden. This garden has at least seven trees. Three giant Ficus trees, a palm tree, two wild banana trees, two smaller trees, and other shrubs and bushes. They are all growing and intermingling. Oh, I have Wi-Fi. The squirrels chewed through the wires the other day, and it took five visits by different crews to fix this. But fixed it was. I am not a technophobe, but neither am I with the latest technology. I am more with the ancients. I value things that last – quality over quantity. I value sustainability.

The name of my house also denotes a place in India. One day, I might go there. I haven't been to India yet. It's one of the few places I have yet to visit. Also, most of Asia, Africa and America come to think of it. I have travelled a fair bit. But I need to do a whole lot more of it and I plan to do so extensively. And bring home small tokens and gifts from my travels. This makes my home an eclectic home. Infused with many mementos from different cultures. Not an anthropologist's home but a psychologist's home. As such, not only the meanings matter but also the life purpose of the items I surround myself with. And the same goes for the people.

I enjoy listening to music. I love it. It lifts my spirits, and it brightens up my soul. I have a great sound system which can turn up the volume for the neighbourhood to listen in on my music. Sometimes on a Sunday morning, I turn it up. As my house has a kind of a church window. It looks a bit like on anyway, and the light streams in through it. It's a constant reminder of our connection to a higher power. I just like dancing, though. When I listen to music, it makes my nerve pains go away. I have some pains from an old neck injury. This impacted the left side of my body a little. Sometimes I slightly limp. It's not too bad though, but my balance is a little off. Nothing would stop me from dancing, though. When listening to music in bed, I like listening to music from movies the most, as the great composers of our age share their deepest feelings. It's so incredible – such music.

As mentioned, and I will say it again, I just love it!

But what did it really take to find myself? Lots of angst. Agony. Pain. And lots of interactions with others. As I am nearing the end of the age of my fertility, I will mostly focus on the men in this book. The men I have crossed paths with, and the men who have come and gone, who have influenced and shaped my life. My friends have done so too, and they will appear throughout as a permanent feature. We are ourselves through our interactions with others. *Umuntu ngubuntu ngabantu* is how the South African saying goes. That is *Ubuntu*. A person is a person through other persons. And we most love those that make us happy, that bring out the best in us. So, it is in community with others, that I found myself, different versions of myself – over and over again. And yet, we have an essence, a true self, a constant that resides within us, our 'self'. This is important to protect, to nourish and to value.

I wish you, as I wish myself, much life.

At this age, I am just over forty. I am feeling the rhythms of the earth, and the rising of the moon, the setting of the sun. I have adjusted to these cycles. I am trying to live a more authentic life, in a valley with people and horses. Together with my cat, Tiago, and hopefully soon, together with my man. I am close to missing it, missing my fertility, and missing having children. That would be a tragedy for me. I have lived a life, and I have learned a lot about what it doesn't take to have children. So, I will share with you.

How not to have children, a guide.

Also, what it means to live in my world?

Agenda at this house:
Human growth and development psychology
Sustainability and climate change eggs
Equality and liberty gender and women's studies
Communication and self-expression art
Spirituality and religions in moderation
Anti-racism and advancement of black people
Peace building and anti-war efforts
Interdependence and interconnectedness
Family, fun and the pursuit of happiness
Trauma counselling and life purpose
Freedom of association and liberty
Power balanced with love
Anti-poverty towards prosperity
Financial empowerment, equitable distribution and opportunities for all

Lifelong learning, travel and cultures
Animal rights and spirit-soul awakenings
Children's happiness, safety and education
Nature and wild animals' spaces in balance
Tech, innovation and insight
Health, wellness and movement body
Food and sustenance: no meat
Chaos theory and physics
Pagan and nature systems and beliefs
Indigenous rights and values
Philosophy, politics and psychology
Economics and history
Futures thinking
Humanism

Chapter 2

2. The accidental rape (Aiden)
And no sex for five years

Disclaimer: This content is not for children. Sensitive readers might want to skip this and the next chapters.

First of all, I would strongly advise to any person who wants to have children to avoid being raped, even if accidentally, at the height of fertility. That is what happened to me at age thirty something. I was together with a man who was rather large in the private sphere. This matters. Because one night, both of us were overly enthusiastic in bed. And I accidentally sustained an internal injury. That is to say, the tip inside of my vagina was suddenly raw. Yes, it is possible. And it happened to me. The man was not to blame. He had no intentions of doing me an injury. It just happened. But I will tell you what it feels like for a woman. Or rather, what it felt like for me. I was super raw, and my homoeopathic doctor prescribed me some white placebo pills to make me feel better. Yes, I went to see a lady who lives in the forest and who believes in faeries. Because I couldn't face my regular medical doctor with these new facts.

What it felt like was the following. The vagina has an ending inside. If it is even slightly raw, it tingles. This feeling goes on forever. It's extremely frustrating. The tip needs to grow back, and that is how it does. I think. I am by far no medical expert, so don't take my word for it, but that is how it felt to me. It took a long time for these sensations to pass. And to regain a sense of normalcy. It was probably what made me run around my garden screaming. And this led to the police coming around to my house. Taking me out of it and hospitalising me in a mental institute for six weeks. Anyway!

But back to the accidental rape. I was in a caring relationship. In hindsight, with more of a friend. His name was Aiden. He looked like a tall Asian, Persian, white and mixed-race type person. A type of god. We met at a friend's birthday party. At a chocolate studio, we were making some chocolate creations in some sort of workshop. It was fun. We were all relaxed. We had a few giggles, a few laughs. We eyed each other out. Somewhat cautiously, somewhat casually. We exchanged numbers. We met again. We had dinner at an Indian restaurant. It was brilliant. We chatted away into the night. We stayed together.

So, what went wrong? And how did it get to the point of an accidental rape? It was an overly enthusiastic encounter after a brief separation. We had by then been together for six months. I had briefly gone overseas, to Berlin and to Amsterdam. In search of... something. What I did in Berlin was I trace the steps of the Holocaust (sorry) through visiting the Holocaust memorial, the Roma and Sinti memorial and the other dedicated memorials. Also, the Berlin Wall, and my family, divided by the wall. What they had in common was they both drove a Lexus. I will always remember that. The family from the northeast, and the family from the southwest. What I did in Amsterdam was I found a fair-trade craft store. And a world photography exhibition, as well as many decor shops participating in a city-wide Elle inspired exhibition, and an olive oil and bread shop. I almost went into the Anne Frank Museum, but I was distracted and put off by a very long queue. When I went home, I shared the horrors of what I had seen with Aiden. He told me that one of his relatives had been a victim of the Holocaust (omg). This was a terrible discovery for me, and I felt awful. However, this frank exchange strengthened our relationship, and after much talking, we blossomed as a couple.

We did weekends away. We went to Stanford as a couple, stayed in a lovely bed and breakfast place. We walked along the streets, and the river, explored the little town and found a couple of retired artists living there. We went to Robertson for a weekend, went wine tasting, and lunching and spent time at a dam. We spent a weekend camping in Darling with friends, during a theatrical festival where people put on shows and invited us into their humble homes. We went to stay with a friend on a golf estate for another weekend, his best friend, actually, who happened to be black. We practised our golf swings, watched videos and had a good time together.

Aiden was a vegan, and I was happy to go along with that as more of a pescatarian. He had morals and values and believed in sustainability, permaculture and building a better world. His mother was Buddhist. He could see the way. He had his own business in installing grey water systems. He had vision. He had gone to the best of schools. She was highly educated. Interesting, thoughtful and kind. He made me think about politics, life and love. He was a great person. Aiden was also a believer in the future of South Africa. He wanted power for the black people. He wanted the bad legacy that apartheid left behind to be overcome. For poverty to go away. For people to live.

It's funny, but it also needs to be mentioned that in South Africa, there is a high incidence of rape. I do not know why this is the case, but I think it's a combination of coming from a history of violence and oppression, mixed with a lack of education and other social ills. I think it needs to be talked about a lot more.

Whenever it happened that I started to feel the rawness on the inside, literally, I broke up with the poor man. He walked away, and he met his future wife two weeks later. So, perhaps it was all meant to be exactly as it was. I, however, didn't have sex for about five years after that. The first year and a half were simple for healing purposes. Thereafter, I was fine, but I just wasn't meeting anyone. It was so terrible. I was isolated and lonely. Even tinder didn't help. All that materialised there was a three-month virtual friendship with somebody else.

After my unwanted absence from sex for five years, I really needed it. I longed for it – to feel a warm embrace, a gentle touch, to be stroked, to be held, to be loved. And not just for the sake of having sex and pleasure. But for the sake of having children. Of course, I didn't want it to be with just anybody. It needed to be with somebody. And somebody special.

And then this happened.

Chapter 3

3. The alcoholic (Andre)
And intimate partner violence

Andre walked into my life.

Out of the blue, after my "nun" period, I got a call from a man I had known as a youthful person. We had dated for a month before my gap year overseas. I remembered how we had been together in our late teens and early twenties, respectively. Andre was a passionate soccer player in his youth. He was a computer literacy teacher. A very good looking one. Anyway, he phoned me. And we started a thing.

Andre came to visit me all the way from a farm in wilderness in Cape Town. At first, I was flattered, later, I realised it was because he was technically homeless and had been asked by his family to please move on. It was lovely to have someone stay. I let him stay at my house. I thought I knew him; after all, we had dated before. I knew he had a sketchy past, and I had visited him in a rehab facility in my mid-twenties once. So, I knew he had once had a drinking problem, but he assured me that this was no longer the case. In fact, it was still the case. He was fully alcoholic. To say he ruined my life would be to put it mildly. Within the next year that I let him stay with me, Andre managed to crash my car, almost killing himself, go to jail for that, and make me lose my job due to intimate partner violence coming from his side. It was so bad. And I couldn't get him out of my life for ages. It was terrible. A best friend of mine who had briefly worked as a drugs counsellor mentioned to me the idea of co-dependency. Yes, he had made me co-dependent within a short space of time.

So why did this man have a hold over me for so long? He kept putting on a most charming act. He wrapped me around his little finger. He used sex to get his way. It was great, trust me. It was even phenomenal; we were a match like no other. We had an insane chemistry. We wanted each other. And yet, the dark times were sad and lonely. When he had his moments of violence, they were intense. Even severe. He strangled me completely to the point that I had permanent lacerations on my neck. And I was always so careful to put cream on my neck to avoid getting wrinkles in my older age. He also hit my head with his wristwatch, which left my head with an injury that sounds like a crackle on the inside when it acts up. He beat me, he hit my back, he threw me on the floor, and he pushed me against walls. All at various occasions. It was extremely violent. I was in absolute denial and always thought he would never do anything again. When Andre attacked me, his eyes changed. He was like a man possessed by a demon. Eventually, I managed to persuade him to move out and to move on. He still bothered me for weeks and months afterwards.

I tried to make friends with him. Andre was incredibly deep. I craved his attention. I realised I needed to give him up. The lows were too bad, and the highs were not worth it in the end.

Love should not hurt. If anyone ever tells you otherwise, don't believe it. That is all.

Why did I stay with him for so long? He was deep and intimate in a way that most people are not. He wasn't shallow. Andre pondered life. He shared his thoughts and feelings. He was endlessly charming. I felt sorry for him. I even loved parts of him.

But it wasn't enough. He was a sick person. Not only an alcoholic but also a mentally ill person. At minimum bipolar, at most schizophrenic. I observed him in very different mental states. I knew he needed help. I tried time and again to get him help. To see a psychiatrist and to get into another rehab. But he wasn't having any of it.

So, I let him go.

I let go of our walks on the beach, building sandcastles, of cooking Mexican tacos and meals together, of hours of watching videos, of going out for drinks, of braais and coffee in the mornings. I let go of self-sabotage and injuries; I let go of pain and suffering. I just let it all go. And let him go.

Besides, this man already had a child. A young son he had to walk away from due to his alcoholism. Something he only mentioned after months of being together. Andre was a formidable liar. One thing he did better than anything was tell tall stories and lies. It was almost on a sociopathic level. I understand why the mother of his son made him leave and forced him to sign the child over to her at a young age. I hope he does one day recover and get to meet his son. I know he longs for him. Perhaps he will if he ever gets better. Perhaps not. But these futures are out of my hands. And out of my mind.

And I hadn't yet given up. I still wanted to form a family. With a man. Another man. I wanted something else.

Chapter 4

4. The interlude (Jamal)
And a daring escape

It's amazing the range of people you can meet on social media.

For a while, I made friends with people from all around the world. So, for example, I made friends with a girl from Myanmar. When the military took over there. She reached out to me. She needed another friend. We chatted briefly at times. She shared on social media what it was like to live with the military junta all around them. Then, when the novelty of the situation gradually wore off, she returned to herself. She liked clothing and accessories websites again. She made herself pretty and started to live her life as best as possible. She was in some situations, but she got through them. I don't know what the situation is like right now. But from a human rights perspective, it was terrible for a while. The military there brutally attacked the civilians after their violent takeover of the country. An atrocious situation to face. I pray for this girl. It is no longer possible to look away.

Then another random person I met through social media was Jamal. I can't remember why we originally made friends. I think we had a chat after commenting on a news article. Anyway. He was a military man, a sergeant or a colonel in Afghanistan, working with NATO forces. As a collaborator, his life came under threat when the Taliban took over Afghanistan. The US and international forces left suddenly. They were withdrawn by the then president of the United States. The local forces that had supported them were under threat. Some left the country and were given safe passage, whilst others remained. The thing is that there was some confusion around what was happening as things were happening. I was texting with Jamal as events unfolded and the takeover began. I realised that there was no chance, and the Americans had left. For a while still, they were fighting back. The men left behind. But the others were too strong and soon took over. At some point, this guy was on his own. I said to him, "You have to take off your military uniform and change into plain clothes." I asked him to do that in order to save his life. If the Taliban had gotten hold of him on his own or even with just a few men, like with his brother, they would have executed him or them. So, he did it, he changed into plain clothes and went into hiding. One night, Jamal received a phone call, and his life was threatened by the Taliban.

He had been directly threatened. After a while, he and his brother decided to leave the country.

Jamal and his brother got out, and through a perilous and treacherous route, made it all the way to Turkey. They stayed there for some time before making an attempt to get to a refugee place in Germany. Some of his friends he had made along the way made it. He said they treated the people well there. Unfortunately, he hasn't made the journey yet. And is still lingering in Turkey, unsure what to do. All attempts to reach out to international aid organisations and government agencies had failed. He was a man deserted. However, he had not yet lost hope. And so I kept chatting to him in a friendly way. I hope he makes it, but I do not know if he will. It's a sad situation. He made a daring escape. And yet his life still hangs in the balance. Meanwhile, in Turkey, there were massive earthquakes that claimed the lives of thousands of people (insane). Those were natural disasters. As houses and buildings collapsed, people were buried under the rubble. Many died. Some were saved. Such situations are heart-breaking. But we have witnessed many natural disasters, ranging from earthquakes to storms to raging floods, in the global world. The news is always just a step behind these events.

I have many journalist friends. It's another life to be a reporter and to deal with trauma constantly. As a psychology student, I am considering trauma counselling as one of the things I could do in the future. I don't know how the journalists cope, quite frankly. But they do somehow find solace in their own lives and recover through connecting with their networks. Some last a while and then opt out. Choosing another life. And yet I am grateful for the news and the media content we receive and can access when necessary and required.

To be honest, I don't even have a television at the moment. I only consume media through my mobile phone and my laptop. So perhaps my view of the world is a little different. I do watch the latest movies and have access to, for example, Netflix. And I have many apps installed on my phone, so I am always on. Just in a different way. I think it throws up some moral and ethical dilemmas witnessing events. Not to merely be a bystander but to actively intervene and to help is becoming more of an obvious need and responsibility. Of course, as regular citizens, you have only limited powers. But exercise those powers you should. For what are we as humans, if not humans ourselves? Making a difference to even one life is important in this day and age. I encourage activism, I encourage participation and I hope for creativity and innovation.

As for Jamal, I hope he finds the resources in himself and through others to make it and to live his life. I am staying in touch to see how the situation unfolds. But beyond that, why did I give so much of my time to this person? Why did I volunteer to become almost like his personal secretary? Researching all the possible channels that he could ask for help from. And sharing this information with him. It fulfilled a deep need to help that was within myself. I will admit to this. I had a fantasy about being protected by a military person. Although nothing ever happened between us in that way. It was merely a friendship. I will continue to pray for this man. And so many others like him.

But, back to main issue of this book. It's probably not the most constructive way – to try to find a man, to spend so much time on those who are unavailable and inappropriate as the potential father of your future children.

It's how not to make children one-oh-one.

Chapter 5

5. The orphan girl (Chloe)
And finding a safe home

Of course, there is making children, and then there simply are children that are already in existence.

I happen to know a girl, since the age of four, who lost her mother to breast cancer. She is now eight years old, and she has turned into the most delightful and wonderful little personage. I am actually so in love with her. And her name is Chloe.

At first, her grandmother adopted her, then after four years, it was too much for her, and she passed her on to her aunt, the sister of the girl's mother. Chloe is so attached to her grandmother. She can't understand why she left her with her aunt. Who is not the most mature or grown-up person? I am deeply concerned actually because the aunt is not really a mother figure but more of a teenager herself. She has a baby and a young son of her own. Luckily, Chloe and her cousin get along like a house on fire.

My role as a kind of family friend has its limitations. I present gifts on birthdays and at Christmas time. I have helped the family financially. For a long time, the grandmother was in my mother's employment as a domestic worker. And I developed a friendship with the family. A social worker was called in by the family themselves to assist with the situation. And with the transition from the grandmother to the aunt as the primary guardian. The aunt is now the legal guardian. I am thinking of asking if I could be a godmother. It's not the same as being a legal guardian, but it's one step closer.

In South Africa, there are also a number of dynamics, including racial dynamics (of course). After all, we live in the post-apartheid era. Chloe is a mixed-race child. And I am actually also mixed race but perceived as 'white'. Technically, I am white plus a tiny bit Asian plus Sardinian (from Italy) and from France, as well as mostly from the modern German and Baltic indigenous. So, it's a pretty mixed bag I would say. But in South Africa, there is the weight of apartheid to carry (sorry), and it's resting heavily on my shoulders. I was previously classed as "white" but I hardly believe in that concept any more. And yet it's in others' minds and hard to get around. I think the best thing to do is to always have a positive approach to everyone and to see others as potential friends. I know there is a lot to make amends for. That is not the only motivation I would have to potentially offer to take on a child. It is love for Chloe in particular.

She is talented, gorgeous, lovely, kind and deserves a better chance at life than what is currently available. At the same time, I am hesitant to offer to take her out of her biological family. I wouldn't want her to cut ties. Her original family should still be able to access her, in my view. I know it might be complicated. But so it is. Chloe likes dancing; she loves her ballet classes, and I would also introduce her to modern dancing, for example. I would have so much to offer her. Or any daughter of mine.

I always had a desire to have children. I had a fantasy to have my own daughter and to name her Siena Lina. Not on my own. I always wanted a father for my children. To be in a loving relationship. I think fathering is so crucial. And it's a big topic right now in the South African society. It's really being encouraged. As it should be.

In fact, I just got a voice note from Chloe. Asking me to please help her to stay in her current school. Her school fees are overdue, and they are harassing the family to pay. Naturally, teachers need to get paid. It is important. My brother is a school teacher abroad. He teaches children math, English and German. As with all teachers, they also have bills to pay and need a roof over their heads and food in their stomachs. They act with love. They give care every day. Teachers are wonderful.

Oh, I am so conflicted about what to do. Do I just assist financially? Invite the girl and her aunt, now guardian, to lunch every now and then. That is what I have been doing. Or do I offer to take her on? As a godmother, or, dare I say, as a mother? That is the question of the moment. Perhaps only if there is a need for it. At the moment, I am taking more the wait-and-see approach. It's a sensitive issue. Of course, it's largely up to the child.

What does Chloe want?

And what constitutes a safe and happy home? Is it the absence of danger and fear? The presence of love and care. Probably a combination of those things.

Chapter 6

6. The ex from ten years ago (Kian)
And exploring true love

Oh, and then there is true love. A once in a lifetime love. The greatest love of all. Love without boundaries. Love that goes beyond. Love that encompasses all things.

I am a being in love. A reminder that the state of love is similar to a slow descent into madness. Losing one's mind is not the worst thing that could ever happen. As I should know, one's eyes go squinty, and the brain goes foggy. One can focus on nothing else but the object of one's affection. Crazy love, insane love, obsessive love and true love. All these types of love exist. Infatuation, a phase, a liaison. A grand love, a slow love, a burning love, a kind and caring love. A love one has waited for, dreamed of, thought of, and wished for. Undying love. Forever love. Eternal love. And most of all, true love.

So that is where I am at. A return of my true love has happened.

I let this man go a long time ago. I wanted to see if he would come back to me. I whispered, I love you, to him one morning as the sun shone on his face and he was barely waking up. I don't think he heard me. He had said "I love you" to me only once. When we were making love, sitting up, our hearts facing each other.

His name is Kian. It means dark. Like the dark forces of the universe. Dark matter. He has olive skin and looks like a boss.

Well, he looks French. He is so damn attractive to me. I don't even know where to begin and where to end.

Some info on our past relationship...

We met at a friend's birthday party at the age of twenty-seven. It was at the waterfront. We were introduced, and there was an instant attraction. Kian made his enquiries and invited me to a dinner with friends after that. He wore a white shirt as crisp as can be. We went out after the dinner at home. For a few drinks and a walk about the town. He put his hand on my leg, and he stared into my eyes. We hadn't kissed yet. Not that night. We shared our first kiss at a major dress-up party. I was dressed as a lioness. He came up to me from behind and started kissing my neck. He turned me around, and he gave me a proper, mind-blowing kiss. I was absolutely in love in an instant.

We shared a strong bond of friendship and of love. We did all the usual things couples do. We watched Planet Earth for hours with his roommate. And we went out to clubs and to friends' parties. We had dinners with friends. We were fully immersed in each other's lives. We went to music festivals and to trance parties. We loved each other. It was unbearable to be without him for too long.

His parents invited us to go abroad with them on holiday. We went snowboarding in Verbier, and we travelled to visit a friend of mine in Lausanne, Switzerland. We did a romantic weekend in Paris, France. We walked up Montmartre to see the cathedral of Sacre Coeur. We went to the Louvre together. We sat in a café, looking bored. Kian was always too cool for school. We had studied the same thing. We had both been to advertising school. We were on the same wavelength.

I really like his family. Like me, he had two parents and two stepparents. Also, he had a sister and a half-brother. I have an older brother. The family dynamics were a match. His mum had once had a bad car accident in which she lost her left hand and part of her arm. Kian didn't mention it to me. Not even before meeting his mum for the first time. I was a bit shocked but recovered quite quickly. I was just as nice as I could be. My mum had also suffered an ordeal. In her car accident, she had totalled her car after crashing into a truck. She had smashed her face on the steering wheel and sustained a bloodshot face which lasted a while. At least no other damages, though. Life, we both knew, is precious and short. And must be taken seriously.

At some point, we had a few fights. We didn't survive these. Kian broke up with me and immediately hooked up with a girl I also knew. A mutual friend, sadly. It broke my heart. We actually got back together. He lied about having been with anyone. I found out through another friend. A phone call. It was humiliating. To have been so betrayed. Kian and I were too young to handle it. I immediately quit my job in Cape Town and took on another offer in Johannesburg. I hoped he would follow me.

He decided to follow in the footsteps of his uncle instead and move to New York. He went across with another girl. When that was finished, we chatted online for six months. We couldn't stop talking to each other. At some point, we lost contact. He must have met many others there; friends and lovers. Then he met his future partner. An Australian girl. She was pretty much perfect for him, and they were together for the next ten years. He had blocked me, and I couldn't even reach him anymore. It was sad for me. I was sore and disappointed. I kept dreaming of him all the time. He would visit me at night. I would wake up with a glow around me; a warm feeling of love. His love still touched me.

It had been true love. But he wasn't there anymore.

The crazy thing is that I went to a fortune teller in Joburg. An eastern European lady chain-smoking cigarettes in a dark little room. Her name was Magda. She foretold me what would happen in my life. First, she told me a lot about my life. Things that I hadn't told her and she couldn't possibly have known. It was like she knew things about me. She told me many things. That there would be a man in my life who wasn't that good. And that I would be with my love. She said Kian would return. But not what to do when he did. The prophecy was one of true love in my life. It was him. She had no doubts about it.

I was distraught. I didn't know what to do with myself. Was I to wait for years?

Chapter 7

7. The sperm donor (Noah)
And potentially, being a single mum

Could I wait for years?
    Or did I just want to have children. By myself. The answer is pretty much a no. Being a single mum is just too hard. But I thought, *I would entertain the idea.*
    Only.
    What would it take for me to make a child with a sperm donor? What would I want to know about this person? I set out to develop a type of census questionnaire and imagined what answers a potential candidate would have to have picked. In order to be considered.
    So, here's the questionnaire:
    Social identity questionnaire
    - Tick all that apply.
    i.e.
    Global / international / regional / gender / age / sexualities / occupation / profession / nationalities / racial / ethnic / national / faith / abilities / class / urban level / relationship status / lifestyle / health / family dynamic / mobility / languages / media and literacy / location

    [International]
    - Closest city (please specify)

[Regional]
- Region (please specify)

[Gender]
- Male (whole world)
- Female (whole world)
- Another gender (whole world)

[Age]
- 0–4 years
- 5–8 years
- 9–12 years
- 13–17 years
- 18–21 years
- 22–25 years
- 26–29 years
- 30–35 years
- 36–39 years
- 40–45 years
- 46–49 years
- 50–55 years
- 56–59 years
- 60–65 years
- 66–69 years
- 70–75 years
- 76–79 years
- 80–89 years
- 90–99 years
- 100–105 years
- 106 years and older

[Sexualities]
- Cis
- Lesbian
- Gay
- Bisexual
- Transsexual
- Queer
- Intersex
- Asexual
- Another sexuality (plus)

[Occupation]
- Scholar (primary)
- Scholar (secondary)
- Student (tertiary)
- Self-employed
- Employed
- Unemployed
- Retired

[Profession]
- Profession (please specify)

[Nationality]
- Please specify (whole world)
- Other nationality (stateless)

[Racial / ethnic group]
- Please specify (whole world)

[Religious]
- Baha'i
- Buddhist
- Christian (Orthodox, Catholic, Protestant, Lutheran, Anglican etc.)
- Confucian
- Hindu
- Islamic (Sunni Muslim, Shia Muslim)
- Jainism
- Judaic (Jewish)
- Shinto
- Sikhism
- Taoist (Daoist)
- Zoroastrist
- Indigenous faith (whole world)
- Spiritual (African)
- Spiritual (Egyptian)
- Spiritual (South American)
- Spiritual (North American)
- Spiritual (Australian and NZ)
- Spiritual (Asian)
- Spiritual (European)
- Spiritual (Russian)
- Spiritual (Indian)
- Spiritual (other)
- Atheist (whole world)
- Other religious (rest of world)

[Abilities]
- Any disabled (whole world)
- Any mental health issues (whole world)

[Socioeconomic levels]
- Low socioeconomic level
- Low to medium socioeconomic level
- Medium socioeconomic level
- Medium to high socioeconomic level
- High socioeconomic level

[Urban level]
- Urban indigenous
- Urban compound
- Urban rural
- Urban farming
- Urban suburbs
- Urban townships
- Urban city
- Urban sustainable
- Urban alternative
- Urban other

[Relationship status]
- Single
- In a relationship
- Married
- Divorced
- Widowed

[Lifestyle]
- Low exercise and movement
- Moderate exercise and movement
- High exercise and movement

- Other exercise (please specify)
- Vegan
- Vegetarian
- Pescatarian
- Meat
- Other food (please specify)

[Health]
- Healthy
- Living with a chronic condition

[Family dynamics]
- No children
- Child 1
- Children 2–3
- Children 4–5
- Children 5 plus

[Mobility]
- Low mobility (infrequent travel)
- Low to medium mobility (occasional travel)
- Medium mobility (occasional travel)
- Medium to high mobility (frequent travel)
- High mobility (very frequent travel)

[Languages]
- One language
- 2–3 languages
- 3–5 languages
- 6 plus languages

[Media and literacy]
- Low media and materials use
- Low to medium media and materials use
- Medium media and materials use
- Medium to high media and materials use
- High media and materials use

[Location]
- In country of birth (located)
- In transit or arrived (displaced, refugee, asylum seeker)
- In another country (in exile)
- In another country (temporary, emigrated)
- In another country (economic migrant)

So maybe. If he got all the answers "right"? Or formed somehow an interesting proposition.

Maybe.

A visit to a sperm bank might not have been out of the question. But the social identity questionnaire was more like a first screening. A second glance would require a closer look at values.

Would it be possible to also make a values questionnaire?

The day I met Noah, I knew I had found gold. He was my potential sperm donor. Rather than looking at various completed questionnaires and choosing a baby daddy off a piece of paper, I was facing a man I knew would be a perfect father to my children. An uninvolved one. But a perfect donor.

Why was he the most suitable candidate?

I met Noah at the supermarket. We literally tried to grab the same bag of vegetables at the same time. Our hands were knocking into each other like fists. Then we smiled at each other.

Apologised to one another. We introduced ourselves to each other, and we exchanged numbers. The thing is, as I found out later, this man spends most of his time cooking vegetables over a fire. He spends his time in the wilderness, as a wildlife and nature photographer. He isn't ever at home. He has a deep need to answer the call of the wild. He has a huge following on Instagram. He is a well-known and renowned photographer.

We had a few lunches and dinners together. We realised we were a match. But not suited to a life together. Another one that got away. But not quite. Not without offering to be a sperm donor for my children.

I said I would think about it... and left it at that.

In the meantime, I dug deep into my mind and searched high and low for any male figures that might still be lurking in the depths of my brain. I came up with the following.

Male superheroes -
The Wolverine
Man in Scenes of a marriage
Dracula untold
Batman
Manor in Black Panther
Sherlock Holmes
Lover in Stealing beauty
Rycroft Philostrate in Carnival Row
Jan Alexander in Goodbye Lenin
Captain America
Spiderman
Antman
John Garret in Greenland
Dead pool
Nick Fury in Captain Marvel

Wilee in Premium rush
Paul Atreides in Dune
Aragorn in Lord of the Rings
King T'Challa of Black Panther
Tristan Ludlow in Legends of the Fall
John Wick
Young Charles in X-men
Young Magneto in X-men
The falcon
Jake Sully in Avatar

And that was it. Those were my go-to guys. My fantasy men. These who had made it into my imagination.

I lingered there for a while.

Chapter 8

8. The luck of the draw (Phil)
And choosing a man

Back to the values proposition.
    And choosing a man.
    My man would also need to share the following base values, I realised.
    I am…
Anti-rape
Anti-murder
Anti-expulsions
Anti-genocide
Anti-war
Anti-racism
Anti-sexism
Anti-inequality
Anti-poverty
Anti-climate change
Anti-unemployment
Anti-slavery
Anti-colonialism
Anti-Nazism
Anti-Stalinism
Anti-all other isms
Anti-apartheid
Anti-killing

Anti-corruption
Anti-theft
Anti-isolation
Anti-misinformation
Anti-propaganda
Anti-inflexibility
Anti-intolerance
Anti-stagnation
Anti-injustice
Anti-arrogance
Anti-greed
Anti-vengeance
Anti-hate
Anti-conflicts
Anti-war

I am also...
For love
For diversity
For tolerance
For equality
For liberty
For democracy
For justice
For sustainability
For fairness
For benevolence
For integration
For life
For mobility
For migration

For movement
For travel
For home
For fair trade
For freedom
For accountability
For responsibility
For cooperation
For agreements
For friendship
For relationships
For marriages
For connectivity
For information
For sharing
For generosity
For charity
For change
For purpose
For innovation
For humility
For patience
For diligence
For kindness

And did I ever meet a man that met these basic requirements?
Yes, I did.
And this was a fisherman from Alaska. His name was Phil. again, maybe not the most practical choice. And I only had a few weeks with this person. A fleeting meeting of minds. A communion of bodies and souls.

I met him on New Year's Eve. At the castle. We were dancing. I was there with a friend. We were absolutely up to no good. We stayed awake the whole night. At dawn, we went to the beach with these three men we had met at this party. The best beach in all of Cape Town. There we lay, gazing up at the sky, the rising sun tingling on us. The day progressed slowly. The next day, we went to a concert at Kirstenbosch Gardens. It was a great concert. We loved every minute of it. I was in Phil's arms for most of the duration of the concert. It was like the music flowed through us.

We were in sync, and we knew it. I would have married him on the spot. Eloped together. But after only a few weeks, he decided to go back home, to honour his travel plans, and to make his way home to Alaska. There, he had a boat and worked as a fisherman. He had chosen that life, and he wanted to stick with it. And so it was.

Phil and I stayed connected on social media for many years, but nothing else ever came of it. We had shared the same values, and yet... it wasn't meant to be.

But I developed a questionnaire for any other candidates to complete. And here it is.

> Questionnaire for self-reflection:
> What have I done myself?
> On racism?
> On climate change?
> On gender?
> On sexualities?
> On crimes?
> On mental illness?
> On drugs?

On homelessness?
On poverty?
On politics?
On faiths?
On professions?
On family?
On social?
On travel?
On languages?
On culture?

Chapter 9

9. The children of Lalela (Grace)
And living an artistic life

So, when your heart has been broken, shattered, even several times, what do you do?

I know I went through some dark times.

I was on the verge of becoming an artist. A full-on-full time painter. I grew up with a stepmother, Daphne, who taught me how to draw and paint. She was an artist herself. What do you do, as an artist, when the one thing you wish the most for is love?

The answer is simple. You give love.

And so I did.

I decided to volunteer at Lalela. An organisation that provides art classes to vulnerable children in the bay I live in, Hout Bay. A small town with a harbour of its own. I went to a local school and gave of my time.

The main teachers were incredible. They were so giving. The teacher that took me under her wing was Mihlali. She taught with a fierce passion. She played games with the kids. Every afternoon. And I was only there once a week for some weeks. The holiday programme was filled with energy and bubbliness. The children were excited to be there. They wanted to learn, and they had a hunger for discovering new ways to create, and make things. There were many children there, boys and girls ranging from age six to age twelve. They had such personalities. Individuals each unique in their own way.

One girl I totally became inspired by. Her name was Grace. She would greet me so nicely. With a huge smile. She was talented and brilliant. And why shouldn't she have been?

What motivates a person to give of their time?

It's altruism.

I am writing a thesis about volunteering and altruism this year. This task is literally on my doorstep. What I have to do is three interviews with voluntary participants. Then to transcribe these interviews. Write a literary review and put this all together. Of course, have some kind of base premise and present my findings as well as come to a conclusion. It's going to have to be twenty-five pages long, with 1.5-line spacings in between all writings. I am actually strangely excited at the prospect of writing this thesis. It's going to be an interesting time.

But back to my time at Lalela. I realised after a while of painting and creating things with the children that I really wanted to draw and paint myself again. Like properly. Not just as a hobby but pretty much full-time. It's a dream I haven't realised yet. But I did recently buy another easel.

And that is a good start.

When I wasn't being creative myself or dreaming up ideas, I would relax and watch movies.

Here are some of the movies I loved in my life so far.

Some movies I loved:
Avatar
Avatar way of water
Legends of the Fall
Eat, pray, love
Babel
The tree of life

Before sunrise
X-men
Black Panther
Wakanda forever
Girl interrupted
The Lord of the Rings
Six underground
The giraffe
Hidden figures
The tree of life
My best friend, Anne Frank
Everything everywhere, all at once
Inception
A United Kingdom
Under the Tuscan sun
Stealing beauty
August rush
Taken
Man on fire
Blood diamond
The constant gardener
Forrest Gump
A beautiful mind
Eternal sunshine of the spotless mind
Top gun maverick
How to train your dragon
The life of Pi
Raya and the last dragon
Before sunset
Twelve years a slave
American history x

Star wars
The matrix
Amelie
The descendants
The best exotic Marigold hotel
Slumdog millionaire
Fatherhood
Respect
Wonderful world
Women of the movement
The sun is also a star
Love at first kiss
Far from the madding crowd
Somebody I used to know
Tolkien
Sideways
Peter pan

Living an artistic life requires input. And output. So, it's only a fair exchange to take from movies and music and to create when feeling inspired.

There has to be a state of flow.

Chapter 10

10. The tinder fire (Daniel)
And not wanting to emigrate

Whilst dreaming of becoming a full-time artist, I met another man on a dating app.

This man was an artist himself, employed as a technical drawer at a good company, in Hamburg, Germany. We chatted on this dating app for a while. Then we moved to a texting app, and chatted some more. About life and all kinds of things. He shared with me that he loved all things technical. Daniel had the best sound system in the world, and he had recently acquired a puppy. He loved this ill pup like nothing else. Above all else, he had a great eye. An eye for drawing, an eye for design.

Daniel also had a love for wild gardens with indigenous plants. His garden was a dream of wildflowers. It inspired me to start going to the local nursery and buying, then later planting some more indigenous plants in my own garden. I then discovered a group of bees had made a hive behind a rock in a wall in the garden. I got further information from a beekeeper, and he advised me to simply keep the bees if they were not in the way. I decided to do so.

My house thus has not only a herb garden but also a small active bee hive. It is, in a way, an apothecary's home. At least. At most, it is the home of the guardians of power.

Daniel, being based in Hamburg, soon asked me when I would return to my country. And when we would meet IRL in real life? I couldn't answer him. After all, I had spent most of my life in South Africa. And only a few months in Hamburg, although it is the base of my family and ancestral home. My heritage is German mixed with a few other things – some French, Italian and Baltic influences as well. Daniel was about to be sorely disappointed. I wasn't ready to leave South Africa yet. I still had much to do here. So it was with a heavy heart that I had to admit that I wasn't coming.

I was staying.

In Cape Town. I hadn't built a home for nothing. I didn't have an original photo of Nelson Mandela in my house for no reason. I wanted to participate and contribute to my society. Not that it was always possible or always easy. Not that I was particularly patriotic, or nationalistic. It was something else. A sense of having a home. A home away from home even. A place to call my own. My house and my home won this round. I didn't know where to go abroad, even though I had a number of connection points. Hamburg in Germany mostly.

It was a long time ago that I had spent some time there. I wanted to go back, no doubt, for a while, for an interlude. But not forever. Not yet.

I remember Hamburg from when I was a young girl. My grandmother greeted me at the airport. We took the bus to her house. She lived in a row of houses in Langenhorn. She had only a bicycle at that point. My aunt came past to say hello and to welcome me. My grandmother always offered me too many chocolates. At other times, I went abroad with my mother. As a child, I spent some time with my cousins and my brother there as well. We visited the black forest, the islands in the north together. As a teenager, I went to the theatre saw the Phantom of the opera, the musical Stomp! And listened to various classical concerts with my family. We celebrated birthdays and other special events. My grandmother made a special rhubarb dessert. She knew how to tell a story. Maybe I got that from her. Telling a story. But I was still far away from finding a man.

Chapter 11

11. The man abroad (William)
And the naked pics

In slight desperation, I thought, *Why not look up an old flame?*

One of the first people that came to mind was a man I had met in London. We had a brief romance, a liaison, whatever you might want to call it. An affair even.

We met at a bar, and we hit it off immediately. I was only twenty-one years old. He was black and he was beautiful. He was quite a lot older than me. His name was William. He too was a photographer, but with a focus on life and humans rather than on wildlife and nature. He took me around the city with his scooter, and he inspired me a lot. I read Zen and the art of motorcycle maintenance in this time. We drank red wine in bars. We chatted into the night. We walked home to his house. He took several naked photos of me on another occasion. They were really good. They made it into his portfolio. With my permission, of course, I remember sitting down and drawing something at his desk the one day. He had some flowers on the table. He photographed that as well.

So, at the age of over forty, I looked him up. I thought, *why not reconnect?* See how his life has been. And as it turns out, he is a successful photographer working for a news agency. He has two beautiful daughters and a loving wife. She is gorgeous. Together, they have travelled the world, and he has published a book on his photography. He became an accomplished person.

So, after this quick check, it was another one to bite the dust, as I was left still searching for a father for my children. It was important to me that we had shared values.

Beyond
Oppression and racism
Sexism and bigotry
Nazism and Stalinism
Genocides and wars
Rape and murder

Towards
Liberty and freedom
Equality and openness
Democracy and systems
Survival and peace
Love and life

Chapter 12

12. The fertility check (mg)
And discovering a low egg count

But was I even able to make children?

It's funny, but I just always assumed I was highly fertile. I went to the gynaecologist recently and decided to check. As it turned out, my egg count was quite low. So, what did that mean?

It meant that I was not a good candidate for a fertility treatment like freezing my eggs. It meant that I might still be able to become a mature mum at the age of over forty. It meant that I was also a prime candidate for adoption of a baby or a child.

But did I want one? The answer was no. I wanted two, or three. A simple or a blended family, any of these would do. After all, what had I done all my family research for? Why had I bothered to draw up a family tree and write up my family story? It was to join the dots to another tree and create a new family. It was to pass my story on to a new generation. And to allow for my children to live a life with fresh energy. Ancestry, to me, was significant only in that it could add some value. Add some insight who could help me out? Make that dream family with me. And would I be able to do this with my one true love?

That was the real question.

And what did I want to do with my life?

What I want to do with rest of my life:
1. Creative writing
2. Artistic creative endeavours
3. Interiors related things
4. Trauma counselling
5. Life purpose and life path counselling
6. Travel more like once a year
7. Be married to the love of my life
8. Write another novella
9. Go to markets etc.

Chapter 13

13. The eventual Dad (return of the true love) (Kian)
And the twins (Siena Lina & Matt Luca)

And then one day, it just happened.

I made contact with the love of my life again. The one the fortune teller had mentioned was my one and only true love. Kian.

Suddenly a window had opened. I was able to reach him, and he returned my call. Our first meeting was at a café called Liquorice and lime. We had briefly met there ten years ago. In between him coming and going to and from New York. We drank three cups of coffee each. We were buzzing with caffeine. He was super skinny and nervous looking. I was overweight from my meds. We were a physical mismatch at the time. This was a year ago. I have since lost weight, and he has bulked up a little. We chatted that day about how our lives had been so far.

Another time, we met at Manna Cafe. We had breakfast together and discussed some ideas. We were into each other, but nothing had happened yet. Kian didn't want to make another mistake. He was in recovery from his last long-term relationship. He said he was recovering from narcissistic abuse. From his former girlfriend. Whilst everything might have looked perfect to an outsider, on the inside, he said he had been suffering. If that was what it felt like to him it must have been so. It was eye opening. I too had believed that he was happy and that he had found someone special. I was even willing to let her have him. I thought she was a great match for him. But he didn't think so any more after a few years together. When they broke up, he took a lot of flak from his friends. They had all wanted to see a perfect wedding and a beautiful life. Those expectations were not met. It was sad for everyone. Friendship was the only thing Kian could offer me initially. So, I said okay.

And we have been "friends" for a year again now. He chats to me every day for hours. He wants to see if we are in line with each other. On the same page. Socially, politically and otherwise. we had many other lunches, coffees and dates throughout this last year. We went to Tasha's, we went to Seattle, and we went to Royale, and so on. We went to markets and looked at various stalls and shops, admiring crafts and collectibles. We chat for ages, all the time. It is incredibly frustrating. There are some levels I just can't get through to yet. Not at this point.

I have suggested to him that we get married, and have two children. Siena Lina and Matt Luca. And the response was something like, it matters that the world around is right. Not a yes, nor a no, just that the world ought to be right, and it's not. As I mentioned in the beginning, something is wrong with the world today, but what is it? And could we solve it together? Perhaps in a meeting of minds and in a connection of hearts. In my mind, it's about making a family together. And loving each other for the rest of our lives. I hope this happens. That is my wish. My deepest wish. But the world is not right.

Kian is a leader – a natural leader. And this needs to come out. He comes from a line of statesmen, painters, stargazers and farmers. I come from a range of professionals, from lawyers to engineers, from ornithologists to traders, teachers and a preacher. Together, we make an amazing match, through the ages, and to the present day. We have in common some French ancestry. We are diverse together, an interracial match, with me being white Asian, kind of, and Nordic looking, maybe Eurasian, and Kian being very French and Mediterranean looking. Looks wise, it's a classic match. He can think, he leads with his heart, and he gives of his soul. He is a good person, even if naughty as hell. He will break boundaries, and keep riding like the wind. I used to ride horses; he rides bikes and snowboards, and has a need for speed. I slow him down, ask him to pause and take a break, and yet get him going again as well. I can inspire him.

I just had some very vivid dreams, actually. My dreams guide me. I am connected to my subconscious. In my last dreams, I was swimming in a clear pool. With mosaics at the bottom of it, and beautiful pictures of people and animals. In another dream, I was following some wild creatures in deep snow. In another, I was doing a presentation on how life could be and as part of the presentation, I handed in a pair of painted leather sandals. Last but not least, I was on a sailing boat, drifting at sea. These are only a snapshot of the kinds of journeys I go on at night. I travel far. I am lucid dreaming all the time. Such inspiration is worth sharing with Kian.

What do I imagine our children to be like?

Siena Lina is a beautiful girl. She is alive and well, and she enjoys being wild and free. She horse rides just like her mother, me. She is turning eleven soon. She loves going to the beach, swimming in the sea. She adores her friends, and she has many of them. She has some funny habits; she won't butter her toast, and she won't eat anything without salt. She is talented in languages.

Matt Luca is a brilliant boy. He is nine years old. He is into motorbikes and has a collection of them in his room. In some ways, he is just like his dad, Kian. He is unpredictable and awesome. He won't give up on his dinosaur collection or on playing soccer with his friends, and he insists on watching MMA fights with his dad at three a.m. in the morning, he is gifted at math. He is sensitive and gentle with others. He beyond loves his cat.

It's domestic bliss. Together, we found and made a heaven.

Chapter 14

14. The other family (Chloe)
And the ultimate happiness

And what happened to Chloe, the orphan girl?

As it turns out, Chloe wanted to stay with her biological family. Where she felt safe. And things would go in the right direction. For her life to turn out the way it should be.

For her ninth birthday, she asked for a unicorn. She got a beautiful horse with wings. Not quite a unicorn, but lovely nevertheless.

The silver lining of this story is that she got to go to a good school and develop her skills in languages, maths and the natural sciences, also in dancing, and in sports and the arts.

Happiness is what you make of it. The ultimate happiness, is a sense of belonging, of being in the right place, at the right time, and with the right person.

Happiness is… love.

In order to ascertain my future, I laid down some tarot cards for myself.

Card reading: 7/1/2020
Tarot cards:
Past fullness
Present core beliefs truths higher consciousness independence
Near future power struggle

Result flow
Hopes personal myth
Opinions and judgement of others
Fears forgiveness
Comment: I was struggling for independence and needed to challenge my mother, which would work out and end well and result in flow, energy balance and new possibilities.

Ancestry stem cards:
Result true love
Feminine energy control
Masculine energy core beliefs
Stem inspiration
Roots truth
Comment: I needed to challenge and needed to gain some control, and look at core beliefs to reach true love. My ancestors were a cause for inspiration and a way to discover and reach the truth about my life.

Question cards:
Sacrifice
Happiness
Personal myth
Comment: There was a question about adoption that was answered in that it would require some sacrifice, result in happiness and build a personal myth as well.

Life purpose cards:
Central innocence
Main aspects judgement choices power struggle
Here and now, true love and holiness flow

End-point sacrifices

Comment: I was wrestling with questions of guilt based on history and what to do to return to innocence, like in an enigma. The main aspects being around facing judgement, many choices and how to achieve a decent amount of basic power in the future. What was required was my true love and personal holiness into the flow of the universe whilst making sacrifices.

Last card:
Vision

Comment: I needed to share visions of my own and help others to find theirs too, as well as share common visions also, this was not only my gift but my true love's as well.

Chapter 15

15. The house (Niaina)
And how to create a lasting home

The thing that I have learned is to take the whole-person approach towards any other person. As a person who studied psychology, I have developed some insights on this. So, what is the whole person approach?

It involves looking at a person from physical, emotional, mental, social, professional, intellectual and spiritual angles. It means taking the entire person into consideration. That is, their health, their emotions, their mental state, their relationships, their careers, their education and their beliefs all matter. in trying to create the life that you want.

I advise people on how to find the path to discovering their life purpose and fulfilment.

One of the tools that I use as part of this process is the enneagram. Through it, a person can learn whether they are more of a reformer, a helper, an achiever, an individualist, an investigator, a loyalist, an enthusiast, a challenger or a peacemaker. Beyond learning what type of person you are, it is possible to connect this to talents and skills and find out what life path is best suited to you.

Another system I developed myself is "visionarie". Through this system, it becomes possible to see yourself in context and discover skills as well as gaps. Filling in the gaps and strengthening existing skills forms a part of living a successful life.

Visionarie works on various levels. It starts with the physical and moves to the metaphysical. It explores the relational, and moves to the metarelational. In the middle is you. The connection point to all things is you. And you can reach out to another higher level, a spiritual level. The physical look at mobility, movement and at home, habitat. Metaphysical looks at innovation, tech and at health, happiness. The relational helps you to learn about power, systems, trade, education and exchange. And the metarelational helps you to learn about people, development, nature, systems. Altogether, this presents to you the person you are in relation to others as well as the person you are within yourself. So, you map out everything in you. And you can see yourself fully and completely.

My home is the house of Niaina.
You are welcome.
What we stand for:
Niaina (global super node)
People (can be great, love, protest)
Anti-terrorism (London, 2005) for sanity
Anti-give (no violence) for safety
Disability awareness (love) for health and mobility
Mental health (psychology)
Anti-racism (for diversity) for rights
Anti-sexism (gender studies) for equality
For sustainability (anti-climate change)
South African (Nelson Mandela and Struggle, id)
And German (family, anti-Holocaust and WW2)
For interdependence (bi and multi literalism agreements)
Lgbtqia+ (friendly, rights mainstreaming, sexuality)

Spiritual (many faiths and connectedness)
With the American (family and development)
And global (trade and relationships)
Indigenous rights (dignity and life, mainstreaming)
Anti-apartheid (anywhere, SA)
Pagan (core underlying beliefs)
And Christian (habits, rituals and traditions)
With the Jewish (family, rights)
Buddhist-inspired (health and wellness)
Aikido (harmony, way of energy, peace)
African spiritualties (all, Ubuntu)
Anti-war and conflict (for peace, and resolutions)
Personalism (MLK, human, dignity social)
Humanism (human development, greater good ethical behaviour)
Existentialism (Frankl, hope and life)
Independence (autonomy, decision making)
Health and wellness (staying well)
Heritage (various aspects)
Location (Cape Town, Hamburg)
Energy (life forces)
Hybrid (identities, futures)
Nature (and wild animals)
Good governance (politics, leadership)
Anti-expulsions (for refugees)
Anti-genocide (anywhere)
Anti-Nazism (for a modern Germany)
Anti-Stalinism (for Russia)
Post-soviet (a more integrated life)
For peace (for global peace)
Anti-colonialism (Africa)

Anti-slavery (global and modern)
Against polarisation (for diversity, politics)
For poetry (writings)
For art (visual, other)
For music (healing, life, energy, vibrations)
For science (learning)
For education (hope for future)
For artificial intelligence (AI)
For technology (intelligent)
For basic needs met (food, shelter)
For family (own, others)
For social rights (social democracy)
For energy (for all)
For integral thinking (for life)
For love (for all)
Protected by the highest laws
Tiago (may God protect)

Chapter 16

16. The world (global)
And what was wrong with it

So, back to the question of what was wrong with the world?
It was a polarisation in US politics.
The left vs the right.
A terrible state, with the centre all but missing. Whilst I had grown up on the centre right, Kian had vacillated between centre right and left. When we met again, he was firmly on the right. interested in financial realities, energy politics and the state of the world. I was going through a phase of learning more about the left, identity politics, freedom, liberty and justice. Kian kept saying if we aren't aligned, we would not have any potential as a couple. And I was not happy to abandon my new found love for the centre left. I wanted to be with the people who were fighting against racism, sexism, bigotry and various social ills. But Kian was focused on other issues. Would we be able to meet and to have civil discussions about politics and life? after he had learned to be as polarised as they are in the US?

My feeling about it was that the centre was missing. Diversity was missing in politics. It was either or, neither nor. There was no range; there was only black or white, blue or red. A disgrace. What makes it worse is that when one side loses, the other side is out of action for years. Instead of all players having a space to play the game. It's a terrible system. one that should be revised. So that there is space for everybody.

My cousin Finn is a councillor in California. He was an independent candidate. For a good reason. He needed a break, and that he got. He does good work. He supports the mayor in his home town. He works hard all the time to deliver services to his constituency and to his people. I am not sure if he even knows this, but our common great-grandfather held a political office as well as a provincial official. In Konigsberg. That was way before the Nazi period. Sadly, Nazism, WW2 and the Holocaust happened there (f*** sorry), and massacres after the Prussian and the Weimar eras, then followed by a Soviet period. Now it's just Russian. Or at least a Russian exclave. During the war, my family was based in Hamburg, or rather, my (our) grandfather was fighting against the French on the islands in the north (sorry). My grandmother was learning to speak English and helped the Americans with translations when they arrived, and the war had ended.

So, now that there is another war involving Russia and the Ukraine, I (we) are disappointed and sad about it. Especially sad is tragic that so many have been displaced and have had to seek refuge. that so many have died, whilst others are left fighting. One of the things that is wrong with the world today is ongoing war and conflict on the global planet. It is war. That is what is wrong with the planet.

What I wish for is a return to peace. but not at all costs. I still want for what is right, good and true to win. I think it's important to fight for what you believe in. for the right to exist: for the sake of defending yourself, for the sake of our futures and our children and for our people. It's important to make a stand, and not to give in to those attempting to take over, those attempting to steal your land, your place, your territory. It's important to defend land, people, culture, and the right to exist. And so, it is.

I have my own ideas about what should be happening in the world. I believe in fighting for independence for Niaina. It should be called Niaina, or the place of no one, and nowhere.

Only then will a balance return. And a lasting peace settle on all the lands around it. The land of Niaina.

That is my belief. it is through:

"Independence for Niaina."

That we shall be liberated and set free.

That we shall be empowered and alive again.

That we shall be awesome and filled with wonder.

Gone would be the days of oppression, the days of being non-existent. back would be hope, freedom, and imagination. Love, happiness and contentment for ourselves and for others. With a return of the indigenous, with rights granted to the same to rule, and others to join in the council. And interdependence to emerge.

So, what else is wrong?

It is the very shape of the world. The world doesn't have enough countries yet. These great empires need to fall. Both the US and Russia need to split into a few smaller countries (wishful thinking). The specifics could be left up to them, but they should be between three to five countries each. It would be the end of an era, and the dawn of a new age.

Also, Kian and I hadn't made any children yet. At this point, time for a break.

Chapter 17

17. The shape of things (Hayley)
and the quantum world

My full name means noble spirit, secret to peace, fertility and beauty.

Whilst I might not be able to change the shape of the world just yet, I am able to change shape myself. I am a (not very) fertile woman, and my body can hold and grow a baby. It is time.

A fertility prayer
I pray to you
With the stones rumbling under the earth
I call to you
With the leaves dancing in the wind
To come into being
With the rays of sun tickling the sky
I ask you
To enter my body and settle in gently like a flower
I guide you
To stay with me as I protect you with my quills
I see you
With my spirit, my body, my soul and in my mind's eye
I dream of you
As you curl up in me like a fern leaf
I know you
As peace settles in all around us through the ether
I appreciate you

As I am grateful that you are within me as sure as a fire
I long for you
With my heart as true as a crystal-clear pool of water
amen

And so I pray for Siena Lina, the vulnerable beautiful spirit, and Matt Luca, the bringer of light, to come into being.
Kian can make it happen.
May the ancestors, the spirit of the time, the dawn of a new age, and the gods of the universe, as well as the quantum world, be with us and protect us.
We would love to make our global super node.
And hope you make yours.
Love, always.

It's not a guide on how to make children. It's a guide on how to make a family and how to love. Find the one and only, the love of your life, and make it happen. Take this from us:
Only those who love are truly free.
For our spirits to unfold, alongside and with each other, together and around one another.

Part 2

Spirit, without borders

About this novelette: "Spirit, without Borders" tells the romantic love story of Kian and Hayley, a couple living in South Africa, in 2027 to 2050 and beyond. It covers the importance of fatherhood, the joy of travelling, setting up their lives, working with various individuals, post-apartheid living and finding happiness in their family. Their children, the twins Matt Luca and Siena Lina, feature as they grow up and come of age and as they navigate life and its various challenges, they find love and adventure, and they live with an untamed spirit.

1. Fatherhood

Circa 2027

And then one day, Kian woke up, his head lying on his shoulder, staring at his wife, Hayley, still asleep next to him, in bed. He knew, she had something growing inside of her – a little one or two.

Kian felt as if his heart was about to burst. He wanted her to wake up, so that he could tell her, wondering if she already knew? She looked as though she was in the middle of a dream, her eyes gently fluttering. He stroked a strand of her hair, and let it gently fall on her face.

"*Mmmm*, well, hello there, darling," he said as Hayley opened her eyes for the first time that day.

She looked in his deep brown eyes and a smile always spread across her face. She loved this man so much and still couldn't believe how lucky they both were to have found each other. Hayley said, "Hey, my love, how are you?" and proceeded to tell him about the dream she had just had. A dream of whales breaching in the sea, the glittering waves at the beach adding an emphasis to the spectacle.

Kian interrupted her softly and said, "I have something to say. I was speculating and hoping. Do you think you might be pregnant? I felt a vibe."

She looked at him, pulled him towards her, planted a kiss on his mouth, and answered, "Yes, I was also wondering about that. Time to do a test."

Ten minutes later, Hayley left the bathroom triumphantly and said to him, "Yes! We are pregnant!" Kian leaped out of bed, picked her up, swung her around and did a little jump for joy. Of course, at that point, they didn't and couldn't yet know that they were expecting twins.

Kian had always wanted to be a father. He had had a pretty cool Dad himself and a decent stepdad as well later. Kian loved children and wanted a little boy and a little girl to teach them about the ways of the world and to show them how everything worked. He loved explaining things, and he loved showing children how things worked. He wanted to be a loving father, seeing his children grow and develop.

"So, then, what should we name this lil one?" Kian asked Hayley.

She said, "I have a suggestion for if it's a girl, but if it's a boy, I want you to name him."

He replied, "Oh, wow, well, that sounds good to me. What's your suggestion, though?"

She said, "I always wanted a daughter to be called Siena Lina. After the town my great grandmother is from."

He said, "Sure, as long as we can add in Rose as well, after my grandmother."

"*Aaah*, that is lovely! Siena Rose Lina for a girl. Yes, that works."

"And a boy? What would you name a boy?"

Kian replied, "I know a few names that I love. Matt and Luca, maybe we could use both of them?"

"Yes!" she said, "and Aslan, after the Lion in the book Narnia. Like a leader with a huge heart."

"Ah, I love that," he said.

"Matt Aslan Luca for a boy, and Siena Rose Lina for a girl."

And they got both. Because they were expecting twins.

Seven months later, Hayley gave birth to two healthy twins, a girl and a boy. They took the twins home to their house in Hout Bay. They lived in a special place, a home almost like an apothecary's. It had a garden with a herb collection on two levels, a loft bedroom, a high open ceiling with beams, and an open plan lounge and dining room with French doors leading on to a patio. It was always filled with light and fresh air.

The cat Tiago was immediately curious upon their return, as they seemed to be bringing some new creatures with them. "Ah my cat, Tiago," Hayley said, "let me introduce you to the twins, Siena and Matt. They are yours just as much as they are mine." because she believed in eco spiritual sharing.

Kian was beside himself with happiness. He was almost in a bit of a state of shock. He wasn't sure what to say any more. He wanted to cry and to laugh at the same time. So, he went to the fridge and poured himself a lemon San Pellegrino. As it was the middle of the day. He took a huge gulp to quench his thirst. Then he walked over to Hayley and said, "I know what you need now. A great toastie made by chef Kian." Then he proceeded to the kitchen, where he made cheese and tomato toasties for himself and his wife.

And then, they hired a night nurse. Because they knew they needed some help. She could stay over in the guest room and tend to the babies at night. Her name was Chrissy and she came from Malawi. The heart of Africa. Somehow, she had managed to get a work permit and she was trained in looking after babies. Whilst Hayley took a six-month break, she knew she had to return to her work later.

Siena and Matt were the cutest babies. They were so open and curious about the world. They were easy to take care of; they were not much trouble. Kian decided to keep a diary about his experiences as a new dad. He made a few notes every day about the twins' progress. And about how he was coping and managing as a father. As a young man with new responsibilities. Fatherhood suited him well. It was as if he was designed for that. And so, the twins grew up, with the loving care of two involved and interested parents and other caregivers, around them.

Chrissy sang songs to the twins when she was alone with them. She remembered her own childhood in Malawi. She had grown up in Lilongwe, close to the lake. Malawi was quite rural and poorer than its cousin, South Africa. She was used to more of a community, and she found the idea of a nuclear family a bit strange. She understood that this family needed her help. And she was willing to give – to share her skills. She was still young, only twenty-four years old, and the parents of the twins were a married couple, aged thirty-seven and thirty-nine, respectively.

She loved how Matt stared at her until she gave him his bottle at feeding times. She adored the cooing sounds that Siena made – the gurgling baby sounds. Chrissy was in love with the babies and in awe of their parents. She also wanted some things for herself, but she was humble and dignified. She was saving up for a place of her own, and although she had a boyfriend, she wasn't yet sure of him as a future husband.

Hayley and Chrissy had more of a friend-like relationship, although Chrissy was an employee. Hayley could not thank her enough and let Chrissy guide and direct her when it came to taking care of the twins. She could not have done it without her. Such are the ties amongst women: complex, interesting, and wonderful.

After six months, Hayley went back to work as a wellness and art therapy practitioner. She regularly held art therapy courses and workshops, at the house. Kian was working under the CEO of an advertising company in Cape Town. Things were going really well for both of them. It was the year 2027.

Somehow, in the years after apartheid, the men in South Africa had taken their powers back. And one of the ways in which this was expressed was through being 'real' men. And again, one of the ways in which this was experienced was by being a father and through co-parenting, or even single parenting. Kian was not the only one on this fathering journey. He was definitely not alone.

Hayley had made some friends through her work. One of them was a young-ish black male single father, around age twenty-seven. His name was Thabo. He was a successful entrepreneur who ran his own bicycle shop and ran township tours in the oldest and most established township in Cape Town. He had a daughter of age seven, and she was the light of his life. It was so heart-warming to share stories and exchange info about parenting.

Fatherhood was indeed not only a trend to be watched but a life phase to be held in high regard. It was about values and about life itself. Passing on a legacy, helping a child to develop and grow into its full potential. To see this potential unfold and to bring out the best in another person. In short, fulfilling human potential.

2. Heart of Glass

Circa 2032

So, some years had passed. And Siena and Matt had grown into little children.

As the twins turned five years old, Kian suggested to Hayley to do an Italy trip to explore her part Italian heritage. She had once done a genetic test to explore her ancestry. She had explained to him in detail how the genetic tests worked and that you could explore various health-related topics through the tests as well.

What was interesting was that, with the ancestry test, you could find out more about the various points of origin of your genetic building blocks. It was through this test that Hayley had discovered she was eighty-nine per cent Western and Northern European (of modern German, French and English descent), five per cent Finnish (of Baltic origin), five per cent Italian (of Sardinian or Tuscan origin), and one per cent Southeast Asian (probably Vietnamese or Thai descent). These results were all corroborated by what she had found in her family tree.

Interestingly, the genetic categories are as follows. They include, but are not limited to these groups. From Europe, there are the groups Western and Northern Europe – Utah residents with Western and northern European ancestry, British and Orcadian ancestry. Of Finnish origin – Finnish. Of eastern European – Polish and Russian ethnic origin. Of South European – Sardinian, Toscani. Of Iberian – Iberian Spanish origin. From

Oceania, there are the groups Bougainville and Australian – Bougainville and indigenous Australian. Of Papuan origin – Papuan Sepik and Papuan Highlands. From Asia the groups are central and West Asian – Haraza, Mansi, Uygur, Kyrgyz. Of Han Chinese origin – Han Chinese. Of South East Asian – Kinh Vietnamese and Dai Chinese. Of Dravidian – Tamil, Telugu. Of Gujarati – Gujarati origin. Of Punjabi – Punjabi origin. Of Dardic – Dardic origin. Of Middle eastern – Druze, Palestinian, Jordanian, Iraqi origins. Of Japanese – Japanese. Of North Asian – Even, Yakut origins. From Africa, the groups are Mande origin – Gambian Mandinka and Mandenka people. Of North African – Bedouin and Mozabite origins. Of West African – Esan people, Yoruba people, Mende people. Of East African – Luhya people. Of San – Khonami San, Ju Hoan North origins. From the Americas – Native Northern American – Karitiana people. Indigenous people of Brazil – Surui people, Mesoamerican and Andean – Mexican, Peruvian, Colombian ancestry. These groups are as described by a genetics research lab. Anyway, do what you wish with these new ideas, as they slowly emerge into the consciousness of modern society. Act responsibly. Back to the story.

Hayley had grown up with her German mother, Marianne, and her brother. She had learned a lot about life and everything else from her. She had passed only a few years previously. Her brother had emigrated to Hamburg at the age of eighteen and joined the rest of the family there. Hayley had a large family in Hamburg; her grandmother had even turned one-hundred-one years old. Her aunt Isabel had passed from cancer at age fifty something. One of the great hopes for genetics research is to have an impact on health management. Hayley's cousins were alive and well, and they had plenty of children.

A holiday in Italy sounded like just the thing, though. Why not? She wanted to return to Venice, where she had been before, for a day, explore Florence, see Rome, and visit the Tuscan countryside, see the artisans practising their crafts, admire the landscape and the art and talk with the people. She had always loved the language, and she spoke a little Italian, also some French, German, and English, naturally. This would make travelling a little easier. She also wanted to go shopping in Milan, and see the fashions and designs there.

A fun part of any holiday was always the planning. Picking and choosing hotels, guesthouses and Airbnb for their various stays. Kian and her spent many hours researching potential stays in the various places they wanted to visit and booking them ahead of time to ensure availability.

When the day of their departure finally came, Hayley was overly excited, her stomach filled with butterflies and her mind turning slowly to jelly.

She put on her amber necklace, a special gift her mother had bought for her in St Petersburg, for safe travels. And they set off for the airport, Cape Town International. An airport known for its short queues and minimal waiting times.

Their first destination was Milan. Hayley's great grandfather had been born there. Travelling as a family of four was no easy task, but it was doable. Hayley and Kian had worked it out; all they had to do was make sure they had enough snacks and entertainment to last for a couple of hours, and then they would be asleep at night anyway. Upon arrival, they went to pick up their rental car. They drove straight to their city hotel and checked in. They had a family room with a main bedroom for the couple, another bedroom with twin beds for the children, and one shared bathroom. What they needed first was a nap.

Of course, once they were up, they wanted to be out and about. And the first place they wanted to see was the Duomo, the Milan Cathedral and the Cattedrale di Santa Maria Nascente (Cathedral of the Nativity of Saint Mary). So, they went there, and walked across the square, taking pics of the majestic cathedral as it rose up against the sun, throwing shadows across the Piazza del Duomo.

There were some street artists, a diverse bunch of people, black, brown and white, dressed in transparent flowy dresses and leotards, doing a dance. It was mesmerising, to say the least. The kids started dancing along, whilst still staying amongst the small watching crowd that started to gather around them.

Kian always took his pro camera with him; Hayley took snapshots with her Panasonic Lumix and was still proud of the 10xzoom. She loved photography, and her photos were good, but Kian had an eye and saw everything slightly differently, in an artistic, forgotten, abandoned kind of way. So, they both took their photos; Hayley's destined for the family photo album, and Kian's intended for his portfolio and potentially a gallery.

Next, they went to the Galleria Vittorio Emmanuelle II to do some window shopping. Famous for its designer, shops this mall was also a masterpiece in architecture. They went into a few shops to look at clothes and designs, and then headed straight for the gelato on offer downstairs. And what a choice they had on offer! Siena and Matt were delighted because they got to choose up to three flavours each.

After that, the family went to the nearest park they could find. As it was a day with some sunshine and they wanted to make the most of that, and besides the kids were getting a bit restless. The next day, they would make an early start, catch an art gallery, probably the Leonardo da Vinci Museum. They had only three days in Milan, and were determined to make the most of it, before moving on to Venice.

When they did eventually arrive in Venice, the children were amazed that an entire city could have waterways as its roads, and that you had to get around on gondolas or little boats. They literally guffawed in awe and wonder. They had never imagined anything like it and were absolutely fascinated. Of course, in Venice, there was the St Marks Basilica, and Doge's Palace to sightsee.

And they went on a glassblowers tour one morning, discovering more about the ancient art of glassblowing. In one of the artisan's shops, a heart of glass was on display. It was unusual, super detailed and absolutely beautiful. "Shall we do it?" Kian asked his wife, looking at her.

"Yes, for sure. I have never seen anything more unique and beautiful than that, when it comes to glass shapes and sculptures," Hayley responded. So, they walked away with a heart of glass, not sure how to protect this beautiful artefact, except for laying it gently in bubble wrap, wrapping it up in a jersey, and packing it in a special bag, which they would still buy somewhere in the shops as they went along.

Then they all sat down in a café for lunch. Paninis with cold meats and cheeses were available, and just what they had in mind, especially for the twins. Today they were pretty wide awake, their attentions having been captured by the artisan glassblowers. Two or three tables further, a fortune teller had made a space for herself. She was charging only 10 euros to tell a fortune. It piqued Hayley's interest. She had spoken to a few such individuals in her life.

Once upon a time, a tarot card reader in Lausanne, Switzerland had told her to go back to South Africa and study psychology there. She had, in fact, done so. Another time, a lady had told her who her one true love was. She was thankful, as she had once had a choice between two men, but only the one is good; this fortune teller had warned her expressly. And she had chosen the right one in the end. Yet another time, a tarot card reader had laid out the cards with respect to her ancestors and told her about her gift in life, which was creative self-expression. She had also mentioned that her grandmother's side of the family was like a council to rely on, and her grandfather had committed a shaman's death and experienced a kind of rebirth in his life. That must have had something to do with serving in World War 2 and fighting against the French (sorry); she could only imagine. So anyway, she was curious.

"Do you think I should go to the fortune teller?" she asked Kian.

"Yes, why not?" he said, laughing at her, a twinkle in his eye.

So, she got up and went over to the lady. "Do you speak English?" she asked her, "as my Italian is not that good yet. And I want to understand everything you say."

The fortune teller responded, "Yes, I am Ukrainian. I speak English. I am a card reader and a fortune teller. I will tell you of your future. Only 10 euros for ten minutes of my time." Hayley nodded and sat down.

"That is your family, yes?" the lady continued.

"Yes," Hayley replied.

"It is good family. It is your source of strength and love. You very creative. You very much understand people. I see," she said.

"Your children. They twins. They very sensitive, good children. They take a lot after you. You teach them how to love life. They always have energy. They are also creative. The girl will make fashion. The boy will design houses. Your husband. He is artistic, too. But he can manage and lead people. He must take the lead. He must make his own business. You are living far from the rest of your family, but you are okay. Do not lose the connection to your family, and to your ancestors. Then you will always be safe and happy. Tell your children also who they are. Who they can be. Any questions."

Hayley was tearing up. She could hardly speak. She half croaked, "Will we stay where we live now, in South Africa?"

"Yes." The answer shot out immediately.

"Never leave that place. It has your soul."

"Thank you, and bless you," Hayley said to her.

Next, she pulled out her cards and picked three. Hayley looked over to the children and smiled at them, reassuringly. She mouthed "love you" and then turned her attention back to the lady. Her name was Anichka. She pulled the heart card, three of swords, which depicts emotions, family, home and relationships, and potentially mental instability and heartbreak. And she drew the queen of wands and a nine of wands. She explained that Hayley's current challenge was to create a routine and find her rootedness. To be grounded in her work, to find her strength and give through her work as an art therapist, and to overcome the daily heartbreak she faced with her clients. Then she too thanked Hayley for sitting down with her and wished her well on her journey in life.

In a way, Hayley thought, the heart of glass that they had bought a day earlier, somehow connected to this reading. She couldn't quite make all the links yet, but felt it intuitively. That was Venice.

The rest of the holiday went by in a flash. It was only a two-week trip, but they still got to discover Florence and its various art museums, as well as the Museo Galileo and the Chianti hills, where they went to visit some wineries. And, oh, so inspiring, Rome, with its Colosseum and the unforgettable Sistine Chapel. There were moments of absolute awe and moments of frustration, of course. The children were surprisingly interested in everything, Siena displaying an early interest in art and Matt gushing over the Colosseum and other buildings, repeatedly saying, "Wow, wow, wow, Mum, look!" to Hayley. Even though they were only five years old. The trip was a pleasure, and they were all super happy.

They ended the trip with a last few days in Tuscany, in an Airbnb house they had rented, where they just spent a few days relaxing, reading books, and swimming in the crystal waters of the stone pool by the house. It was straight out of a romance novel – an experience for a family, never to be forgotten. The only thing they didn't manage to fit in this time, was a stint in Sicily or Sardinia, a trip to explore the culture that inspired the likes of Dolce and Gabbana, the fashions that were marked by white lace, and colourful embroidery, black velvet and other fascinating textiles.

"Kian," Hayley said to her husband on the last day of their trip, "why do you think we have been so incredibly lucky in our lives to be able to live in such a fairy tale?" And she really meant it.

"Oh, I don't know," he replied, "maybe we got something right in one of our past lives," he teased her. "We are very blessed in this life, though, aren't we?" he stated, and acknowledged.

"I have been thinking about it. And I think it's about time we give back. When we return home, I want to look into some creative projects that engage the youth. I've got some ideas spinning around in my head... I am still working on them, but I think I can do something through my work, maybe. Anyway, we'll see what we make of it all when we get home."

And with that in mind, they set off on their way home, back to Cape Town. They couldn't wait to see the photos they had taken, read and enjoy some of the books they had picked up along the way, and display some of the artefacts they had collected in their home. And for the children to be home again, in their daily routines. That was a bit easier, but they had loved every day of the trip and had hardly been difficult or complained. The two weeks had been a joy for all of them. A glimpse into the Italian way of life, taking notes on some ancestral roots, and enjoying the vibrancy of the culture in its modern heyday.

3. The Diplomat

Circa 2034

About two years later, somewhere in Hamburg, Kian and Hayley were staying at an Airbnb. In part, they were visiting Hayley's cousins and their children, as well as some friends and other people they had worked with over the years. The twins were with them, and they were seven by now.

Their visit had begun with a bit of sightseeing for the sake of Kian and the children. A trip to the park Planten und Blomen, a day spent at the new harbour waterfront, and an evening at the Elbphilharmonie were also planned. They had wanted to see a musical like The Lion King but it was fully booked. So, they opted for an evening of classical music at the fabulous new concert hall, Elbphilharmonie.

Of course they didn't have the appropriate attire with them; it was a smart black-tie event. They needed to go shopping for the whole family, and they went to the Alsterhaus on the Alster Lake in the centre of the city to try to find something, anything, that they could wear. They found darling dresses, one for Hayley, in lilac with patches of beige, arranged in semi-leaf shapes, and for little Siena, one in a flowy red. For the men, Kian discovered a black suit with a white shirt, and for little Matt, a cool grey jacket and smart white t-shirt. Now they were ready.

Kian was highly sensitive acoustically, and Hayley had an issue with too loud sounds due to once having had a mental disorder she had struggled with but overcome. It was schizaffective disorder that makes people shield themselves from being overly stimulated and having too much input. Yet both of them loved good music, for different reasons. Kian was inspired, Hayley was healed. So, a visit to one of the most amazing pieces of architecture, built to bring out the best in sounds, was going to be a treat for them and a new special thing for the children.

A variety of classical music was due to be played by the Royal Philharmonic Orchestra, who was using the hall that night. An English concert, in a way. After arriving and being shown to their seats, they settled in and started looking around them, enjoying the view. Siena was too excited. "Mum, what are they going to play tonight?" she asked.

"Ah, you will just have to wait and see. Or you can ask that nice man at the back to look at his programme?" and off she went.

"Sir, do you speak English?" Siena asked the kind-looking gentleman sitting in the row behind them.

"Yes. I speak some English. I am a Russian diplomat, though," he replied. "And how can I help you, little lady?"

"I was hoping I could sneak a look at the programme you have in your hands."

He laughed a loud laugh, and a couple of people turned around. "Did your parents not get you one?" he asked.

"No, we came a bit late and couldn't get one anymore," Siena answered.

"Ah, I see. Well, you are welcome to quickly have a look at the programme."

So, she took it out of his warbly hands and snuck a look at it. "Thank you," she said, and she gave it back.

And the concert began. It was wonderful. A symphony of sounds, an orchestra filling the room with music, and singers filling the air with sweet songs. In the break, everyone filed out in single file into the pause rooms. There was a bar. Kian ordered drinks from a swish-looking waiter. A glass of champagne, a cognac, a Coca-Cola and an ice tea. Siena told him about the diplomat. "Oh, my hat! Are you serious? If only your mother knew. She would find that very interesting," he said.

Matt said, "What what what is so interesting?"

Kian replied, "I will tell you a story tomorrow. Then you will understand. but not now." As Hayley returned from the bathroom, she was greeted with smiles all around and her glass of champagne.

Hayley suddenly stopped in her tracks. "What! I can't believe it. That's Tim over there, my first ever boss here in Hamburg! The one I did the graphic design internship with at his ad agency! We must speak with him," and she walked over like a butterfly. She greeted him elegantly, and he introduced her to his friend, a lovely-looking young black man, and a Portuguese-looking woman by his side, in a pale-yellow dress. "Tim, it is so good to see you after all these years. I always knew you were this classy. But to see you here tonight of all nights! amazing."

"Wow, Hayley from Cape Town! Unbelievable. How are you? Is that your family over there. They look lovely," Tim said, slightly overwhelmed. Then the first gong went, and they had to start heading back. Tim and Hayley quickly exchanged numbers, and she told her how long they were here for. This led on to an invite to a lunch at Tim's house with his family and the same friends who were staying with him on a visit from the US.

The rest of the concert was a stunning ensemble of sounds. The children struggled a bit towards the end to stay awake, but they were glad they had come, for they had been given the option of staying at home with a babysitter or coming along, and they had chosen to go with. Another beautiful evening together.

The next day, they decided to take quietly and enjoy in a more relaxed way. They took a boat on the Alster, cruising around the canals. Matt asked his dad, "So what did you want to tell me about last night?"

Kian looked at him silently for a while, then replied, "Okay, I will tell you a story. It is quite a long story, but I will make it short and sweet just for you."

By now, Siena's ears had pricked up and she slid over to hear better. "Me too; I also want to hear the story," she said. So, he began telling it, with only a silent nod from his wife.

"Once upon a time, there were settlers in a forest. They lived together in medieval times, and they had built a community. Along came some knights, and they took over the community, and the lands. Together, they founded a city known as Konigsberg. The King's Mountain. It has a founding stone a heart of stone. Many years passed, and many wars were fought. It was a kingdom ruled by kings and queens. Your mama's ancestors are from this place. The first one we remember in 1800 something was a farmer. Others were an ornithologist who studied birds and a fur trader who traded in furs. A lady that bought many properties in the city after selling a family smallholding. Lastly, a provincial official. By then, the royals had been deposed of and a constitution had been put in place. A state was born.

"Your great grandfather was born there, but he moved here to Hamburg, where he fell in love with your grandmother, and they stayed here together for the rest of their lives. Together, they faced the savage times that were to come. A dictator took over Germany and caused World War 2. About eighty million people died whilst the whole world said no to Germany, Italy and Japan, who had formed the axis alliance. The allied forces said no. The

Holocaust (Shoah) happened, and millions of people died, six million Jewish people and others were murdered and genocided. This was very sad and tragic. Nothing like it had ever happened before. This dictator was really bad, and his name was Hitler. Only the Soviets could end the war, and they managed to win with a victory over Germany's Nazi side. Your mum's grandfathers were war veterans on the German side (sorry), and my grandfathers were war veterans on the English and French side. So, me and your mama being together is like making peace every day. But you already knew most of that hey.

"And Siena talking to a Russian diplomat yesterday was a bit funny for your mum because she was once almost declared an enemy of Russia. After writing many impassioned letters to the Kremlin and the president about what happened in Kalinska after the war and complaining about the expulsions of the Germans, as well as asking for a citizenship. She was politely told to live in Russia like anyone else if she wanted to and forget about her ancestors. And to never mention to anyone the idea she had proposed to them: independence for Kalinska. As that would have made her a separatist. And can you imagine your mother as a gun-slinging war hooligan? Probably not so much. Anyway, she came around and realised that the world is one anyway, and all of us being interconnected, and interdependent, is far better than causing wars over territories. Even if she had the rights, as they were her ancestral indigenous lands," he said, looking at her with absolute love and teasing her.

Through the alchemical forces of the universe, at that exact moment, their four Alsterwassers arrived at the table on the boat. They were all really thirsty, so it was a good time to drink this lemonade mix. Matt and Siena asked away, threw questions and comments at both Kian and Hayley, including whys and hows, and please explains. This was more than an education. It threw a new light on their mother and the shenanigans she had been up to as a younger person before being married.

That night, Hayley thanked Kian for explaining all of that to their children. When they had gone to sleep, they quietly made love in the bedroom of the Airbnb, with an open window letting the moonlight shine in.

Then the day of the lunch with Tim came around. Jack and Liz were the names of the couple that had been at the concert, and Tamara was the name of Tim's wife. Sara was their little girl, aged nine. She welcomed the twins and immediately engaged them in an activity that somehow involved looking for lemons in the garden. They had prepared a Mediterranean kind of snacky lunch. There was a table spread with a chequered tablecloth, with a vase filled with chamomile flowers and other wild flowers. Tim had always had a soft spot for Hayley, as she had come all the way from South Africa just to do an internship. He had looked out for her as a nineteen-year-old.

Jack was especially curious to talk about South African politics and to touch on the apartheid history. As a black American man, he had his own views on the politics of the day. It was 2034, and there were now several political parties in place that were all pretty solid and grounded in reality, ranging from left to right, but without too many extremes or any major issues. Politics had settled into a constant flow of activities and actions. Kian and him got into an interesting discussion, and Tim was an eager listener. The women, Tamara, Hayley and Liz, split off and formed their own little group, whilst the children ran in and outside of the house as they pleased.

Hamburg was such a great place to discover and to visit, and spending time with Hayley's cousins was also rewarding and interesting. At the end of it all, they flew back home to Cape Town somewhat tired, but they were looking forward to planning their next trip back already.

4. The Girls at the Back

Circa 2036

A bit of time was spent at home. In 2036, when the twins were nine years old, life became quite busy for both Kian and Hayley.

Hayley was working as an art therapist, doing workshops from home. She had an interesting participant, a woman named Gael, who had suffered from an eating disorder. She was on the road to recovery, and she was exploring her self-concept. She started painting a huge candle in great detail, wax dripping all over its sides, and it taking on a beautiful shape as it burned down. Hayley often had clients who painted the most incredible things. It was more than a work of art; it was an achievement in self-expression and in learning to see herself and find a way forward.

"Gael, what does this painting mean to you?" Hayley gently asked her.

"Well," she said, "it represents me as a candle, burning down yet giving light, taking on a new shape yet disappearing, at the same time."

"Wow. And how does that make you feel?" Hayley probed further.

"I don't know; I think I feel a little sad, yet also happy, even content, at the realisation that this is my life," Gael described her emotions.

"Well done. Cup of tea?" Hayley offered, at this point, to take the pressure off.

"Sure," Gael said, and they sat down together after the other participants had already packed up and left. Hayley felt this was the start of a long and deep friendship, and she was right.

Kian was still working at the same advertising agency for the CEO, but he had started making plans to break away and start his own agency with a good friend of his, Vuyo. His friend had grown up in exile, with his parents living in London. He had missed most of apartheid in his formative years, gone to a private school, and at the age of eighteen, decided to emigrate to South Africa, where his parents had originally been born. Somehow, he and Kian had met through work and had fast become friends many years ago. Both were in advertising, yet they complemented each other. Vuyo was a creative director, and Kian was on the business side of things. So, they were meeting a lot and hatching plans to start their own agency together.

"Kian, what do you want this agency to be called?" Vuyo asked him, in midst of one of their many discussions.

"Ah, I don't know; I have some ideas, but you're the creative one, so don't you rather want to put forward some suggestions?" he replied, in a good-natured way.

"Yes, I do have some ideas as well. I was thinking of the Rainmakers. I will explain why. There is a saying that goes like this: 'If you sing to the skies, the rains will come. If you pray to the gods, the plants will grow,' and I think that if we use this as an analogy, we can say that we will make sh** happen," Vuyo said.

Kian responded, "Yeah, that is awesome; I can dig it. I totally feel the vibe. The Rainmakers. We could even have a tagline that goes something like this: Pray with the Rainmakers." and they continued to bounce ideas off each other, throwing various taglines at each other and exploring the idea. It was a good idea.

Before they could both leave their day jobs, to start this agency, they had to get all their ducks in a row. So, they were making plans and figuring things out.

There was still time for a holiday, though, and Kian and Hayley had plans to go to France. A trip to Paris was planned, with a detour to Normandie and the countryside. They flew with Air France, and they arrived safely in Paris. No complications and no delays, they were lucky, as this had almost become the norm on many other trips. They were seasoned travellers.

Upon arrival in Paris, they made their way to their hotel. They had left the twins at home, with Kian's parents looking after them. They were ever so grateful to be able to spend two weeks together as a couple, a luxury they hadn't been able to experience for a while. On their first day, they headed for the Louvre to absorb some art and to admire centuries worth of paintings. At night, they saw people on the bridges skating and rollerblading. They were so free, and so elegantly moving along. They really knew what they were doing. Kian and Hayley went to a local restaurant, and he ordered a steak with Mediterranean vegetables on the side, and she ordered a chicken dish with broccoli and cauliflower stems. For dessert, they shared a crème brûlée, and a delicate chocolate mousse. They were delighted when the chef brought in a lit candle, and the waiters started a rendition of "joyeux anniversaire", as it was Hayley's birthday.

The next day, they walked around Montmartre and went to see the Sacre Coeur church. On the way they stopped at a street vendor's stall to get some crêpes, filled with Nutella sauce. They saw some street artist doing a drawing in chalk, and observed his drawing for a little while. He was very talented, and his drawing became more and more complex as he continued with his work.

They continued on their path, and walked around the gardens close by. That evening, after taking a lazy afternoon nap, they went on a night stroll towards the Eiffel Tower, and saw it covered in fairy lights. It was a beautiful sight to behold.

A few days later, they were headed off to Normandie. They had booked a villa stay in the countryside and a space at a cooking school for Hayley, whilst Kian wanted just to read his books, write notes, and sort his thoughts. The villa they had booked was in fact an old rambling house, with vines growing over the front porch and bramble bushes leading up the walkway to the house. It was overgrown, yet it had been tended to with love and care. Inside the house was a dream of French linen: simplicity mixed with understated farm-style elegance. They settled in, happy in their new surroundings, and they got out the laptop to make a video call to their family back home.

That night, they indulged in honest, raw sex; they craved each other and hadn't had much privacy in years. They were entangled in each other and woke up naked, still wrapped up in one another. Even after years of being together, each encounter was fresh yet familiar. In the morning, they enjoyed just some fresh coffee with cream.

Then it was time for Hayley to go to her cooking class. The Silkworm Kitchen was the name of the school. Hayley was excited and a little apprehensive. Would they accept her? Would it all go well? Sometimes the French people had issues with people of German descent coming to them, especially in light of what her grandfathers had done (sorry). They had fought against the French close to here. So, she felt pangs of guilt, and yet, she reminded herself, she also had some French ancestry from her grandmother's side. So, it was with this conflict in mind that she went into her first class.

Usually, she was the one giving classes, but this time she was a participant, and that felt good. Amy from the UK, Mimi from France, and Lindiwe from South Africa were some of the other participants. They all had to briefly introduce themselves by name and where they were from. They were all keen to learn cooking the French way and to learn more about how to appreciate food and prepare it slowly and well. The school was definitely a part of the slow food movement.

The first meal that they were going to learn to make was tomato bruschetta, followed by French onion soup, followed by braised beef and mixed vegetables, carrots, potatoes and onions. Lastly, they were going to learn to make a strawberry pavlova, still that same day. And so, it went for three days straight, they were cooking up a storm. Lindiwe came to Hayley and said to her, "So I see you're also from South Africa! Whereabouts are you from?"

Hayley replied, "Cape Town, and you?"

Lindiwe said, "Joburg, darling, Joburg, it's the only place to be. I live in Melrose Arch."

"Oh, interesting. I know that place; I used to work in Johannesburg," Hayley told her. "In the old city, on Market Street."

Lindiwe looked at her, slightly surprised, and then said, "Ah, wow, that is lovely."

"Nothing like afternoons at Moyo at Zoo Lake and lunch in Rosebank or Parkhurst. Walking in Emmarentia Park, and so on... Yes, I had a nice time in Joburg; I had many good friends there and worked in consumer research," Hayley elaborated.

"And what do you do?"

"Ah, I am an actress, actually. I have worked on a television series called Young Africa; have you seen it?" Lindiwe said.

Hayley replied, "Oh, I don't really watch television much; I gave it up about ten years ago, but it sounds amazing; you must be so talented."

"What do you do nowadays?" Lindiwe wanted to know.

"I am an art therapist. I work from home and hold workshops," she answered.

"Oh, that sounds great! I would love to do one of those; I have always wanted to draw my heart out." Lindiwe smiled at her, a glow in her face.

"Well, just let me know if you are ever in Cape Town," Hayley offered.

"Yes, I will definitely take you up on that," Lindiwe replied.

Mimi and Amy were also chatting away whilst cooking and were giggling at something or other. It was a good atmosphere in the cooking school. And the best part was, they got to take home the food they had prepared, so they could be real homebodies and treat their stay at the villa as a romantic retreat. Kian was loving his time at the villa. He went for a walk every morning, after a strong cup of coffee, and then settled in to the day. He was making progress, and his notes were all neatly ordered in his leather-bound notebook.

"Darling, I think I have had an epiphany," Kian said to Hayley on their fourth day at the villa.

"Yes?"

"We need to move. We need some space to grow, to be, to exist. Our house in Hout Bay is lovely, but we can still expand and reach our full potential. Would you like to help me to look for another house when we return? Also, it needs to be a place that can hold the twins as teenagers and us as more established people as well," Kian continued.

Hayley responded, "I think it's the next step in our growth

phases in life… and that we should look into it. Yes." And so, with these grand new plans in mind, they started packing their bags and headed home – to their first together home.

5. The Last Kingdom

Circa 2036 to 2045

A move to a new house was never going to be easy, and finding that new house presented even more of a challenge.

Upon returning from their trip to France, Hayley and Kian set out to search for a new home. And they found it within two weeks. A beautiful artist forest retreat in Tamboerskloof, in what is known as the city bowl of Cape Town. This was only five minutes from the city centre, where Kian was looking to start his and Vuyo's agency. Not only was proximity a factor, but the house itself was ideal. It was a lovely old Victorian house that had been opened up and renovated. At the back, it was more like a greenhouse, and it had a studio space for Hayley's workshops. In short, it was perfect, with wonderful trees in the garden and stunning details inside. There was ample space for Matt and for Siena; it was a four-room house, so there was space for a guestroom as well. At the moment, the twins were nine years old, but they would soon be teens, and another life stage would begin. This was a house that could hold them that they could grow in together.

So, they put in an offer, bought the house and moved in within a month. Their original home in Hout Bay was bought by a young couple that had just had a baby, it was their turn to make it their own little paradise. And the new house, they gave a name: Niaina.

After their idea of an imaginary kingdom for their family,

after their hopes and dreams for a place of somewhere, a home.

Hayley continued with her work as an art therapist and integrated wellness practitioner, expanding on some of her offerings and taking on a more diverse client base now that she was more centrally located and more accessible. She started using mixed mediums in her classes and even provided the opportunity for participants to work with clay and make their own sculptural works as well.

It reminded her of when she was twenty-one years old and working in a clay café in Hampstead, London, hosting workshops for children.

Siena was soon turning twelve years old, and she had turned into quite the young modern dancer. She loved her classes, and she was great at performing on stage, shining her light brightly. Matt was of course the same age, them being twins, and he was developing into a very nice young person as well, with a particular fondness for reading comic books at this point. He would spend hours in his room, copying the books, doodling away and drawing his own comics. He was really good at it, and Kian was teasing him to that he would be the next creative director. He said he would take him along to work one day and introduce him to all of his colleagues.

Kian and Vuyo had started the agency, the Rainmakers, in Cape Town. They specialised in television ads and commercials, for which it was ideal to be based in such a picturesque city that held endless photographic potential.

Together, they created and had a good vibe going. Their agency was situated in Gardens.

For some inspiration, Kian decided that they needed to go to London. So, they planned a work trip together. They envisaged many appointments with potential clients and catching up on some trends.

So, it was next stop London. This was Vuyo's home base, where he had grown up. His parents had gone into exile during the apartheid years. He was a black person – to the English people – maybe, and a Xhosa and Sotho person – to the South Africans. His name meant joy and happiness. He had brought much of that to his family, and his sister, Ayanda, had also lived up to her name, representing growth. She had become a lawyer and stayed in London. Whilst Kian was staying in a hotel, Vuyo was staying with his parents during their London trip.

Kian was invited to dinner with the family on the second night in London, in the nice, established neighbourhood Marylebone. He was a bit nervous, as he hadn't met Vuyo's parents before, and besides, he had grown up as a 'white' person during apartheid in South Africa (sorry). As such, he first of all owed them an apology, or at least his sympathies. He hated that he was a former white person, guilty of existing in the worst time. He had been born into a system of prejudice; a system that ran on segregation that was designed to keep people apart. He was always opposed to that, as his parents had been, more from a religious than a political perspective. They had said no to apartheid, but they couldn't leave, as they had only had South African passports at the time. Vuyo had, of course, already told his parents all about Kian and his family, and so they were well informed about their visitor.

Difficult conversations about racism in history as well as iterations of racism in the present day were not to be avoided. Yet at the same time, Kian didn't want to get too heavy, offend or even depress his hosts. So, he decided at first to let them do more of the talking and offered some talking points about his English, Irish and French heritage as well. They politely asked after his wife, and he told them briefly how they had met over twenty years ago. He finally plucked up the courage to say the following: "If you could say one thing to my parents, who were stuck in SA during apartheid, what would it have been?"

The father answered, "Just to hang in there, son, just to hang in there. For things will always come right, and good will prevail over evil in the end." and that had been their philosophy, in exile. Yet they had actively worked against the regime of the day by protesting, being activists, and supporting the struggle back at home.

The next day was a busy one for them. Kian and Vuyo had back-to-back meetings with three potential clients, presenting their agency to them and trying to win them over. They were a client in the banking sector, a client in the energy sector, and a brand in the luxury goods market. All highly desirable clients, and they definitely wanted at least a foot in the door. Kian and another colleague in business development, Mark, had secured these appointments. They were all around town, and they had to use taxis to get to them on time and to find the right places. It was fun; it put them in a bit of a spin; their adrenalin was pumping, but they saw these challenges as manageable and as good. In the end, they won over two of them: the banking and the luxury goods clients. A feather in their cap.

They had a few more days in London, with some of the time spent sightseeing, and amongst other things, visiting the London Eye, and the memorial to the victims of the 7/7 terrorist attacks in 2005. Hayley had been in London then and was almost about to take the tube that morning, yet she had, in her ditziness, overslept and missed her travel connections. A real stroke of luck, a twist of fate. Kian shuddered to think that Hayley might have been on that tube that fateful morning, and then quickly popped the thought out of his mind, as it made him feel simply too uncomfortable. Yet he thought also of those lives that were actually lost and sympathised with them and their families. At this point, he actually wanted to go home again; he missed his wife and the children.

So, without further ado, when the time came to go back, Kian bought Hayley the obligatory magazines at the airport that she had demanded he bring back for her when travelling without her. It was a mix of women's magazines, interior magazines, creative magazines and psychology magazines. She was always very appreciative, and her collection provided much inspiration, also for her workshops. Only a few more hours, and he would be home.

He would move mountains to be back home. His home was his kingdom his home was his domain. He was the leader of the pack, the lion to his lioness, the king. This was all true, and his wife and children affirmed this every day. By giving love, he rose in power. This was their home. He was so happy to return and be in his space, where he could relax, unwind, and let everything drop. He could just be himself.

So, after his taxi had dropped him at his forest house in the city, he walked in and saw Hayley standing there, paintbrush in hand, looking a bit lost, confused, and shy. He was overwhelmed with emotion and felt a tear rise up, his throat constricting. He croaked, "Hi," and she said "Hi" back. They slowly walked over to each other and gave a warm embrace.

"Missed you," he whispered.

"Yeah," she said. They went onto the lounge, where the doors opened up to the garden, and the sun shone in gently.

6. Fate: The Crystal Saga

Circa 2039

As the twins Matt and Siena turned twelve years old in 2039, their parents, Kian and Hayley, were in midst of transforming and taking their work lives to the next level.

Matt and his business partner Vuyo, as well as some colleagues, were headed off to Johannesburg for a gala event. It was an event of a blue-chip client to celebrate their thirty-year existence.

At the gala event, there were many important and well-known people of particular significance in South Africa. Ranging from personalities to business icons and others who had various achievements behind them.

There was only one keynote speaker. The son of a Holocaust survivor. After the first course, the dinner guests were invited to take a moment by the master of ceremonies. Then he introduced the speaker on stage.

"I am going to read you a poem from my grandmother Frances, a Holocaust survivor.

'Another day,
Another life gone.
I cannot speak.
For it is unbearable.
We are sad,
Yet we are in this together.

I hold hope for the future,
That this will end.
My thoughts,
Are with you all the time.
I am safe,
In my mind.
I am whole and complete,
And I am worthy.
I am loved,
And so are you.'

"This poem was written by my grandmother after she was liberated from the Neuengamme concentration camp in Hamburg.

"It demonstrates her sheer will to live, the hope she held in her heart, and the strength of her mind, as well as those of others in the same situation with her. They held out till the end, until they were liberated – those who survived. It is a stark reminder that we must always have respect for life and treat others with dignity. Even in times of war, it is necessary to maintain decency, to hold on to basic values, and to not let anyone destroy you. Only with immense inner strength can such negative forces be overcome and the light shine through. I hope this helps you to understand, and I hope you will honour the victims and celebrate the survivors with me. Thank you for your presence and participation here today."

The audience began to clap, and as the applause grew, people rose to their feet, giving the man a standing ovation.

Kian was close to crying, but he held back his tears. Then it was time for the main course and more conversation. A table near the entrance was decorated with a crystal swan. He realised it made him think of the empire line in Russia. Another world, far far away. He wondered what it was like for Hayley, thinking of the fact that her great grandparents were from what was now a part of Russia, but were previously German. She had once told her of her trip to St Petersburg and the beauty of the Church of the Spilled Blood. The present year coincided with hundred years since the outbreak of World War 2. So many lives had been lost, and the Holocaust (Shoah) had been the most unthinkable tragedy during this time.

And hundred years later, after the end of the war with the Ukraine, Russia and Europe had settled into a new relationship. One based on agreements towards interdependence, as both had realised that they could not continue without each other and an enemy path was not an option. A new alliance had thus been born, and the United States and Europe were okay with this. They were more than okay with this, they were pleased, in spite of the circumstances of previous years of war and aggression. They were willing to give peace a chance.

Kian could not wait to get home and tell Hayley about the gala event. She would have come with him, but she was holding a series of talks herself in Cape Town about mental health and wellness, based on her years of experience as an art therapist and wellness practitioner. Her talks were popular and basically booked out. She even got a few requests to put together a workbook or a mental health and wellness manual. Something she had been thinking about for a while. She could make it really creative with drawings by herself and past clients. She was thrilled with the idea to make such a manual. She loved the manual of "The Warrior of Light" by Paulo Coelho, for example, but that was more based on poetry.

It was interesting to have a conversation with Hayley about

the Holocaust. Her stepfather had been of Jewish ancestry but lived his life as a Catholic person. He had worked for the German government in communications for thirty-five years, after the war. It gave her a different perspective, plus her grandparents were from Hamburg, mostly, and so she had that to think of as well. She always apologised for the Holocaust. The guilt associated with the war veterans, and then she had a Jewish ancestry herself. It gave her a complex, balanced view. When she heard about the Holocaust survivor's son's story and the poem he had read out, she took a few deep breaths and said, "Wow, I so wish I had been there with you, Kian."

"You were," he said, "at least in spirit."

Kian and Hayley had often talked about how to manage such difficult topics with their children. They had opted for an open approach, discussing things, facts, difficult topics, and emotions with them from an early age. So, the twins Matt and Siena were pretty mature, for their age of only twelve, and understood a range of things from a perspective that was well beyond their years.

That year, the family also went on a holiday to Mozambique. The north of the country had been plagued by some jihadi troubles, and the South Africans had had to send in some troops to help as peacekeepers. Many younger kids of Mozambique had evaded recruitment into jihadi groups by feeling on motorbikes, dirt bikes, scooters or anything mobile that was available, even bicycles. Some had taken refuge in some national parks further up north and refused to join in the activities their former friends might have been exposed to.

So, the peacekeepers were able to restore the peace, but the scars of some attacks were still visible in some places. However, as mere travellers and tourists to the country, it was almost impossible to see any of that; there were reports that Kian had seen in the news.

But Kian, Hayley, Matt and Siena, aged twelve, managed to take a beautiful break at a resort near Pemba. It was absolutely stunning – a beach holiday – days spent swimming in clear blue waters, others spent exploring local markets, and walking around the town. They spent two days in the city too, in Maputo, in a hotel, and enjoyed the general atmosphere, and went to a nice restaurant for a seafood lunch. Kian took plenty of photographs, and so did Hayley. They were only visitors, but they felt somehow close to the people – a certain kinship.

Each year, they did something that would generate some inspiration and help them both in their careers and in their personal lives. And this year, it was that.

7. Home for Christmas

circa 2045

A few years later, in 2045, in Cape Town, South Africa, the year was heading to a close, and preparations for Christmas were underway. The family was together, and Kian's relatives, his brother and his sister and their respective children and spouses, had planned to spend this holiday together.

The Christmas tree went up a week before Christmas, and Hayley and Siena decorated it, with silver lametta, original beeswax candles, red baubles, little wooden figurines, little Christmas elves and faeries, and African animals in shweshwe fabrics. It was a kind of hybrid mix of decorations from Germany, South Africa, and the UK. The tree looked impressive, and the star at the top was its crowning glory.

They had a miniature nativity scene made out of clay, and that was a centrepiece on the coffee table. On the lounge table, some angels and more wild animals covered in shweshwe fabrics.

This year would be extra special as it was their last Christmas with the twins as 'children' as they were coming of age. They were due to turn eighteen at the end of December. Quite a summer party was planned for that. But first, a family-inspired Christmas. They had decided that each person would bring only one gift, and each person had been allocated whom to bring something for by drawing names out of a hat at another dinner.

Christmas Eve was also special to them, and they went to

church for that. Followed by a dinner at home, sole fish with potatoes and red and green peppers, with a sponge-type of cake for dessert. Just the four of them sat around the tree for a while, with the candles lit, and discussed some key events of the last year as well as future plans. They ate Christmas cookies and had some special coffee liqueurs later at night.

The next morning, on Christmas day, they woke up quite excited, and looking forward to their guests. From about ten-thirty, the relatives started arriving, first the sister and her family, then Kian's younger brother and his family. They were all so lovely. Hayley couldn't get over it; she felt so lucky to be a part of this family. Of course, the siblings had had minor disagreements here and there over the years, but these had always been worked out. They generally got along well. And their children, aged nine, ten, fourteen and seventeen, respectively, were delightful and were, of course, cousins to the twins Matt and Siena.

Christmas gifts were exchanged, and everyone had a chance to unwrap their present. It was a mix of goodies, ranging from a beautiful bag to a pen, an atlas, a pair of funny socks, a head torch, a fancy lighter, a cookbook, a novel, a straw hat, and so on. There were many laughs, smiles, and giggles at the gifts; some were surprising, and yet others expected.

For the Christmas lunch, they had made it easy this year; they were serving chicken and beef fillet slices, roasted cherry tomatoes, as well as butternut, an aubergine bake, a couscous salad with mixed peppers, and a humus dip and tsatsiki dip with naan flatbread.

They had various cool drinks on the go, ranging from orange juice and Coca-Cola, to ice tea, as well as some white wine spritzers for the grown-ups.

Niaina, the artist forest retreat house they had lived in for the past many years, had come into its own. The patio was sheltered by the shade of trees, and the chairs were arranged haphazardly around a long table. They were dining outside, al fresco, in the cool, fresh air. There was much chatter and talking, and there were pauses, and also lazy silences.

"So," Kian said to the group at the table, "what are your thoughts on this last year? Any highs and lows you want to highlight?"

He continued, "Well, I'll go first. My highs this year were achieving our first million turnover at the agency and starting to write a book. My low was our father passing away. It haunts me, but we all are dealing with that grief in our own ways, I suppose." He sighed and passed on the momentum to speak.

"I'll go next," said Hayley.

"My high was another series of lectures I delivered at the college of psychology. And my low was also the passing of your father, and then that small accident I had where I fell and hurt my knee running. That was a pain." There were some mumbles of shame and sorry.

Next up was Kian's sister, and she said, "My high was getting a promotion at work, and I think my low was also my dad's passing. That was and still is really tough for me," and she looked at her husband.

He was a lovely man, an Afrikaans man with a slight accent as he spoke English and a deep kindness. He said, "Hmm, yes, well, my high was maybe buying a new car, and my low was the same," and there were nods and a silent pause.

"Yes," Kian's brother piped up.

"My high was climbing Mt Kilimanjaro, and my low was being sick for a week afterwards. Yeah, and Dad passing, of course."

His wife picked the next turn to speak and said, "Yes, and me, my high was having the family over for Hanukkah, and then my low was discovering a cancerous mole on my back. That was scary, but at least it's been removed and I seem to be okay now. I just have to watch going in to the sun. And of course, my father-in-law passed."

There was some further discussion and contemplation on the passing of the siblings' father, an event that had occurred earlier that year, in March. He had simply passed away in his sleep at the age of seventy-six – not that old, but after living a pretty decent life with its own challenges along the way. Their mother had passed three years earlier from a sudden heart attack. That had been unexpected. But the siblings were determined to keep the family spirit alive and to get through their grief. Hayley, always with a counsellor's hat on, said, "Grief takes time, and people experience it in very different and unique ways. We all know about the five stages, according to Elizabeth Kübler Ross, from denial to acceptance, with anger and bargaining and depression in between. but it takes a person to uniquely experience it in their own way." And on that sombre note, they changed the topic, and talked of other things for the rest of the afternoon, playing musical chairs, and at times, having intimate conversations with each other as part of a larger group discussion. Further topics were the politics of the day, climate change, social realities, friends and their families and their social network. Some gossip filtered through: did you hear of this one and what that one has been doing, and so on?

The children and teenagers were alternately in the garden and in the house, at the table, and not at the table, depending on whether there was something to eat going, or not. In the afternoon, there were some cakes on the go and desserts. Since they had actually helped to prepare a lot of the food, they were quite keen to try their work. As the afternoon turned to early evening, both pairs decided to make a move and start heading home. They were super happy with the day spent together.

December was always such a busy month because many friends from overseas chose to come back for the holidays. When Gabrielle came home from Lausanne, Switzerland, Hayley had to immediately catch up with her over a coffee in Camps Bay. They also decided to do something cultural together and to go and see the new apartheid museum in Cape Town. Whilst they had both grown up as 'whites' under apartheid, both had rejected this identity or paid little attention to it during that time. They were sorry. They were still, even at this age, coming to terms with the history.

So, this new museum was something they both wanted to see. Hayley had been to the apartheid museum in Johannesburg before, but there had never been one in Cape Town, not for years. A strange oversight, or perhaps due to a lack of resources. So, they went to the museum. There was a black-and-white photographic exhibition there, with photos taken by Jürgen Schadeberg and others. Amazing. It was quite something to be reminded of the pain the past brought to people, especially what had been done to the black and the "coloured" people, as they were labelled, and any other persons of colour. So, it was more a question of paying their respects and acknowledging the past.

And then it was that special day. The day of the twins Siena and Matt turning eighteen years old, becoming fully legal. They were both so excited, and they had invited over fifty friends and even hired a venue for this, a local hall. Turning eighteen was not for the faint-hearted. It came with certain expectations. They had invited their friends, and it was a lovely and diverse bunch of teenagers, mostly kids they had gone to school with, and a few more from other schools as well. The parents were told to stay on call but to stay away, and they were only allowed to bring snack platters and cater for the event, which they did willingly.

They had also hired a DJ to play music, and he played a mix of trance, pop, rock and alternative music. Their best friends were Grace, a beautiful girl, and Danilo, an Italian boy, respectively. So, Siena and Grace had been plotting for ages which girls and boys to invite, and Matt and Danilo had done the same. The girls invited about thirty other teens, and the boys got to invite about twenty. It was fair enough. It was quite a wild party, as might have been imagined. But all went well, and the teenagers had fun, dancing, drinking, some smoking, kissing, laughing, and having a ball of a time. That was another summer down.

Kian had also been helping his friend Stephan, a soccer coach, by filming his young team, and the coach then being able to make improvements to the game and style of playing. Some of the kids playing were from further away, and some came from the townships just to play the game. So, it felt good to give back, and take time to help the coach with insights.

So, there were many things happening that summer, and that Christmas, and their holiday and time to catch up with friends and family were over before they knew it. They were growing and thriving as a family, but they also knew that new adventures were up ahead, with the twins leaving school and starting to pursue their own paths in life.

8. First Love

Circa 2045

Siena Lina and her best friend Grace, a gorgeous (biracial) girl, had decided that they would do a rail trip around Europe after school together. A three-month adventure, time out and time for exploration and travel. Whilst both had been in various places in Europe before, they had grown up in post-apartheid South Africa. Growing up in a diverse country and with poverty always on their minds, they wanted an escape, a place they could go and get to know more people, whilst discovering new places. So, they bought a euro rail pass, which was flexible, and you could hop on and hop off the trains pretty much as you pleased.

They had started out in Italy, moved through the south of France, and were currently in Spain. A few days in Barcelona were on the cards. They decided to start out the day with a takeaway coffee, a pastry, and a visit to Park Güell, with its beautiful mosaics. Once there, they sat on a bench and watched passers-by stroll around. Two young men of a similar age approached them. They introduced themselves and said hi. Their names were Daniel and Thomas, and they were American. They were good looking, both pale in complexion, the one slightly Asian-inspired, the other slightly Viking-looking.

"Can you girls recommend any good places in this city? What have you done so far?" they asked.

"Well, we only arrived last night, so this is actually our first outing," Grace replied.

Siena piped up, "Yeah, we wanted to find some good tapas later; maybe you know something?"

The guys got quite interested in that saying, "Hmm, maybe we can walk together for a bit and find some cool place close by, chat for a while?" The girls agreed and joined up with the two Americans.

They walked for a short while and came across a place that offered tapas. They sat down and ordered a few dishes to share. More interesting than most of the sights were these two young men. Fascinating, their piercing blue and brown eyes, their blonde and light brown hair and their slightly tanned skins. *They were hot*, thought the girls. *Why not spend a bit of time together?* They started telling each other about their lives, life back in South Africa – life in the US. They were both from California, from San Francisco.

Daniel said he was studying law, and Thomas was studying economics. Grace and Siena weren't there yet, but both had plans. Grace wanted to study psychology, and Siena was interested in fashion design. The young men were flattered that the girls had taken out time to get to know them. Before they parted ways, they exchanged numbers and found each other on social media. It was pretty clear from the start that Daniel liked Siena, Grace liked Thomas and vice versa. Quite a lot. The attractions were instant, palpable, it was like a stroke of luck had hit all of them.

Grace and Siena spent a few more days in Barcelona, whilst the guys had already moved on in the other direction, through to France. The girls went to see the Sagrada Familia church, the Barcelona aquarium (they weren't sure why, but it seemed like a fun thing to do), the Picasso Museum, which they absolutely loved, and lastly, Las Ramblas for shopping. There they bought, altogether, one black and white striped jersey, one red dress, one lilac and one floral patterned dress, brown sandals, a pair of green kitten heels, and two bikinis for the summer heat. Not too much, as they were travelling, but just enough to infuse their wardrobes with a bit of Spanish style. Whilst they hardly spoke a word of Spanish and struggled at times to get directions, they managed to find their way around quite well.

Suddenly, they got a message from Daniel. "Lovely ladies," it began, "we were very taken with the two of you and would like to invite you to join us at Thomas' grandparents' cottages in Stockholm, in Sweden, for a week, if you are keen. No expectations; just offering this out if friendship and hoping that you will say yes. This could be any time next month, we are flexible."

The girls looked at each other and squealed. "Whaaat, that is insane! how mental," Siena said.

"How dope," Grace said. "I want to do that. I really liked Thomas, the blonde dude, and I could tell you had a crush on Daniel, the semi-Asian guy. Listen, I think we should do it. Head up north, go to Amsterdam, Berlin, Hamburg and up to Copenhagen, then Stockholm. What do you think? I know it's a mission, but that's what this holiday is all about, right?"

Siena replied, "Yes! For sure! I am so totally amped. I can't believe they asked us! what fun!"

They wrote back, accepting the invite and providing an estimated day of arrival.

And then they followed the plan and went to all of these cities, all the while secretly looking forward to their last planned destination the most.

9. A Perfect Story

Circa 2045

When Grace and Siena finally arrived in Stockholm, they were ready for a holiday from this holiday. They had maybe seen a bit too much, travelled through a few too many cities, and they were a little tired. They needed some rest and relaxation. So, they arrived at the cottages that Daniel had promised them they could stay in that belonged to Thomas' grandparents. They stayed in a cottage called Aurora, and next to that was another cottage in which the young men were staying, called Linnaea, after the twin flower Linnaea borealis. Whilst the first cottage was named after an aurora borealis, a natural display of lights flashing across the night sky. The cottages were close to the lakes. It was an idyllic setting, a perfect place to unwind for a few days.

Siena had taken her camera along, and was happily snapping away. She had an eye for photography, a talent from her father, Kian.

"We want to take you out for coffee today, please," one of the guys said to the girls, and they agreed. It was an iced coffee with a difference that they were presented with in the end, at a local cafe. It was like this. Into a giant ice cube, a hot espresso was poured, which was at first to be sipped with a straw and then dug out with a spoon as it turned to sludge.

They were chatting and talking about South Africa and growing up there. Grace took it upon herself to educate the American boys a little about apartheid, and made them promise that if they ever visited Cape Town, they had to go to visit the District Six museum, a tribute to a neighbourhood that had been diverse and integrated and had been destroyed in apartheid times (f***ing hell). Grace told them that her great grandmother had been born in District Six and had been forcefully removed along with the rest of the people there. She had still lived a resilient and interesting life and managed to overcome the difficulties and challenges she was dealing with. And she had made a family; Grace's mother was her daughter, and they had grown up in Woodstock. So, Grace told them of their experiences, and Siena told them of hers as well. Her family had objected to the apartheid regime back in the day, supporting religious leaders and others who were in opposition. They were not really a part of the struggle, but they did object and had ways of not participating in the hate directed at black people in particular. So, they had been friends of the struggle, in a way.

What was more recent were the Black Lives Matter activists that had, however, turned out to be quite Marxist from an economic perspective. So, whilst they wanted to support them, they had other economic models in mind, especially Thomas, who was studying economics. They discussed the history for a while, and realised that they were just lucky to be beyond those times and to live in a better time, a time where social democracy had taken hold, at least in Europe, and economics was based largely on free market economics. So, the conversation drifted from one topic to another, and they discussed a whole range of things.

That evening, they decided to do a barbecue at the cottages. They pooled some foods they had left in the house but also did a quick trip to the shop around the corner, which sold some basics. They had collected fresh rye bread, some spreads, sweet potatoes,

potatoes and a few other root vegetables, onions and lettuce, tomatoes, cucumber and feta cheese, for a Greek salad. Also, some meats for grilling of lamb and beef varieties.

As night fell, the stars came out and started softly twinkling in the sky. They had eaten a wonderful meal that they had put together themselves, and they were now about to roast some marshmallows over the remaining coals. It was such a romantic setting; they actually made a few jokes about it. That night, Grace and Andrew got together, and Daniel and Siena also did. It was a double match made in heaven. Or double trouble, depending on how it would be best described. Whilst the girls were both eighteen years old, the young men were aged twenty and twenty-one each. A match, if there ever were one.

Grace and Andrew retreated into the one cottage, Aurora, and then the other two were left sitting outside by the fire for a while. You could hear some commotions as things were heating up a little, as they had moved beyond kissing to more interesting things. A pot seemed to have fallen to the floor. Siena was feeling a little shy at this point, but Daniel said to her, "Come, let's go inside," and so they did.

She was now in the Linnaea cottage, and it was such a perfect Scandi-style wonderfully decorated cottage inside, it made her feel at home immediately, just like Aurora also had, which was almost identical. "It's funny, you know, because we are staying in these twin cabins, and I actually am a twin myself. Did I mention that to you yet? I have a twin brother, Matt. He is super cool," Siena said.

Daniel replied, "Oh wow, no, I didn't know that. How interesting. What is it like to have a twin? I have a younger sister and brother, but no twin."

Siena said, "Well, we get on like a house on fire. We often

have the same ideas at the same time, and then we have this thing where we go like, 'Snap!' You know?" she was laughing. At least the ice had been broken. And the rest, as they say, is history.

And that was their trip to Europe. They had travelled far across the continent, zig-zagged all over the place, they had experienced over nine different cultures in nine different countries. They had been in the south, the east, the west, and the north. They had met Ukrainians, Russians, Spanish people, French, Italian, Americans, Africans, people from the Netherlands, Germany, Sweden, Hungary, Croatia and Italy. They really had tried to cover many bases. And they had enough photos to create all kinds of memory boxes and photo books. Their exposure to the various places and people left a great mark on them. They felt changed. But what had probably changed and impressed them both the most were their encounters with the two young American men. Would they ever get to see them again? They wondered as they boarded their planes home, heading back to Cape Town, South Africa.

10. Happiness for Beginners

Circa 2048

In 2048, the twins Matt and Siena were to turn twenty-one years of age. Whilst they were both at home in South Africa, Matt had chosen to study and learn about architecture in New York. And Siena had decided to pursue her interest in fashion and textile design in Cape Town. Her best friend, Grace, was studying psychology at the University of Cape Town. They still hung out all the time, even though they were at different schools, and they had many shared friends.

As one of her projects at the fashion design school, Siena Lina made a print with lions, trees and a crown, based on elements from her family crest and on her ancestors. The local meaning of the ancestors was significant; much emphasis was placed on the history and background of a person. Siena knew this, and she was also inspired by many textile designers from around the world, who often used a combination of heritage, local culture, and imagination.

Siena was very talented in her designs and in drawing fashion designs. She had picked up a number of special art techniques from her mother, Hayley, who was working as an art therapist for many years. Their home, nicknamed Niaina, was the centre of their familial activities, and she still loved going home, although by now she had moved into a shared apartment in Gardens with another girl friend, Busisiwe. This friend was studying as well she was at an advertising school studying marketing and advertising communications management. She was a feisty, fun girl who had great self-confidence but also a sensitive streak. They got on well, gave each other enough space, but also cooked together often and shared meals in the evenings. They had a student routine, and it worked for them.

Tonight, they were making a chicken Caesar pasta salad. Thereafter, they were going out to a new gin bar and a live music concert. Matt was going to join them. He was visiting from New York and staying at home for a week-long break. He came past and joined them for dinner at the apartment first. He was the designated driver for the night. "So, what have we here?" he asked when he saw the delicious looking salad.

"It's a chicken Caesar pasta salad, just the way Jules, recommends you make them," Busi replied.

"Jules, who?" said Matt.

"Jamie Oliver's wife," she retorted.

"Oh right. Well, it looks delish," he said. And they began to dish up the salad. They had some further chit chat with Matt, bragging a little about all the amazing street food and restaurants he had been to in New York so far.

Then they headed to the gin bar. There they were met by Grace and another girl, Lucy. The five of them made a good-looking little party. "Wow, it's been a while," Matt said to Grace as she joined them. "You look... amazing," he continued. Grace did a double take as he saw Matt as well. Was this the boy she had known since the age of seventeen? The same one? Siena's twin brother. It seemed to be so. Sparks? Could this be sparks flying?

The drinks menu at the gin bar was incredible. It offered a variety of gin cocktails and gin spritzers. Alcoholic and non-alcoholic options are great because Busi refused to drink alcohol.

So, she opted for a non-alcoholic gin-mix drink. Lucy was a lovely girl who was a university friend of Grace's. She was also studying psychology and English literature. She was a fiery redhead, kind of Irish looking, and also attractive. Matt was spoilt for choice, but somehow, he couldn't take his eyes off the Grace he had thought he had known so well. She had turned into a real stunner.

By the time they got to the concert, it was obvious, even to Siena, that something was happening. Some chemistry had been released, and some magical forces were at play. Grace and Matt were into each other. Lucy, Busi and Siena gave them a bit of space, as they intuitively felt that they needed some time alone together. Even if they were in a crowded room. About to watch a live concert – a small gig, but a fun one.

And so, their story began.

Later, Grace would say, it must have been the gin goggles, as a joke. And Matt would say, it must have been that red lipstick, in response. Because they didn't end the evening there. Matt went home with Grace that night to her apartment in Tamboerskloof, just up the road from his family home. When he wasn't home the next morning, he phoned in sheepishly so that his parents wouldn't worry. He made Grace and himself a great cup of coffee. They sat in the morning sun, looking at each other. "Quite a night," Matt began.

"Yeah," Grace echoed. She was not confused any more. She was in love. He was smitten.

He simply said, "So, what now?" and they talked for a short while.

They decided that morning to give a relationship a go. Even if it was long distance for a few months, until they could properly be together. Matt had another seven months left in New York. He invited her to come and visit him there too. And so, she did.

New York was a city like no other. As an architecture student, Matt had been to see some of the most interesting and significant buildings in the city. He lived in Greenwich Village, and he got around on buses and on the tube, with taxis as well. Most of all, he enjoyed walking around the neighbourhood, an artistic yet down to earth place with many restaurants and interesting shops. Grace wanted to take in as much as she could in her short visit. She was only there for a week. So, they did the Statue of Liberty cruise, rented bikes and rode around Central Park, did a Brooklyn tour, went to the Guggenheim Museum and the sea, air and space museum, as well as to the site of the twin towers, also called Ground Zero. They were not that into PDAs or public displays of affection, but they did enjoy holding hands and sometimes kissing in public. It was love.

11. Spirit Untamed

Circa 2050

In 2050, the twins Matt and Siena were twenty-three years old. Matt had returned from New York and been together with Grace for over two years already. He had finished his architecture, and she had completed her psychology master's degree.

There was a wildness in Matt, though, a restlessness that was untamed. His spirit needed to be released somehow. He thought of going to Botswana and proposing to Grace there. He knew they were both still quite young, but he felt that this was the person he wanted to build a life with. He just knew. So, he flew her to Botswana, to a game reserve called the Moremi game reserve. There, you could witness the miracle of the Okavango delta, a delicate ecosystem. Matt was prepared; he had a ring from his father's mother's side, the British side of the family. It was a family heirloom passed down for generations.

Matt was nervous as hell. He knew Grace could have anyone she wanted, but she had hinted at staying together forever before. But still, he was taking a huge risk. He needed to consult with the spirits, and what better way to do this than to stare into the fire at their camp the first night they arrived. It crackled and burned, and the flickers and flames were starting to look like animal shapes to him. Was he hallucinating a little, or was he just anxious? He called his mother, Hayley, later that night. She reassured him that everything would be fine but urged him to keep an eye on his mental health to take notes.

He decided to go deeper. He felt he could find his spirit animal by looking into the fire. So, he went back outside and sat down again. He needed it now. So, he closed his eyes and started more to feel the fire and sense the energies around him. He saw it now. His spirit guide... it was a cheetah. An elegant, fast, flexible and beautiful creature. And he had a vision. Of a few cheetahs interacting and playing together, and one suddenly getting lost. He had to find the lost one, and so he did. He realised suddenly, what this meant. He had, in a way, stolen Grace from Siena, and she was feeling a little lost without her best friend, even though she had plenty of friends. He needed to make it up to her, and yet he simultaneously had to pay as much attention to Grace as was required. For a couple in love. He had to resolve this. His twin sister, he needed to speak with her. Suddenly he saw another cheetah on the horizon, and then he understood. There was someone waiting for her. He had been there all along, but he hadn't been able to get to her. He knew now what to do.

The proposal was well planned. He was going to ask her after dinner in their chalet the second night. He had a little speech in his head. That day, they went on a tour of the delta and saw plenty of wild animals in action. It was an adventure. They had a great guide; her name was Mpho, which means gift. Dinner was perfect. Everything was perfect.

After dinner, they went to the chalet, and he found the moment to go down on one knee and present her with the ring and the question, "Grace, will you marry me?"

She was a little taken by surprise and hesitated. "Wow, Matt, I wasn't expecting this. I am not sure what to say..." and she covered her eyes. "Matt," she continued, "I honestly don't know..." She started crying a little. "Sorry," she whispered, "I didn't want to ruin it, but I can't say yes," and she turned around, and got into bed, pulling the covers up around her. "Please come to bed," she said, and she waited for him to join her. "I can't. I don't know why. I just don't think marriage is for me. Not yet anyway." She cried some more, tears starting to stream down her face.

Matt was honestly shocked; he was not sure what to do next. He got into bed, as he had been ordered to do so, and lay beside her. He felt sad.

Disappointments are not easy to deal with, and this was the greatest disappointment of Matt's life. He had been so sure, and yet she had not been on the same page. The next three days together were a bit of a blur, but they had a chance at least to talk everything through, and to learn more, and understand each other better. Grace felt they were still too young, and in fact, she was too old for him to marry him. She thought, *somebody's wife should be at least five years younger than them.* She couldn't change this deep-seated belief. It led her to believe that she wasn't 'the one' for Matt. That he should keep looking. He could disagree as much as he wanted to, but it wasn't going to change her mind. A frustrating and disappointing situation. And yet, they had loved each other deeply and been together for almost three years. At this point, they decided to split up, yet remain friends. Matt was released.

His spirit was broken. He felt like his life line had a break in it. He needed to spend some time at home; he needed to speak to his father, Kian.

12. Ninety Minutes

circa 2052

At the age of twenty-five, the twins Matt and Siena had grown into fine young adults. After his breakup, Matt had thrown himself into his work at an architecture firm in Cape Town. In fact, they had an opportunity coming up for him in Johannesburg, albeit only for a project. He accepted the opportunity with gratitude. He had always wanted to spend some time in Johannesburg, especially after his time in New York.

Matt Luca, as he was known to his friends, had established himself as quite the talented architect. In Johannesburg, he made some great new friends. Sebastian, who happened to be black and from the UK, an asset manager in the financial sector, Graeme, a business manager at a tech company, and Sipho, an environmental consultant in the energy sector, were amongst some of his friends. Together, they made things happen.

Matt had been right, though, with his vision. There was a man waiting for Siena. It was the American guy she had had a holiday fling with in Sweden. Daniel, the American, suddenly contacted her out of the blue. He had big plans to come to Cape Town, and was she still there? he asked her on a social media platform. She was stoked to hear from him. Yes, she was still in Cape Town. He had finished his law studies, and he was keen to travel. Would she mind if he came to pick her up, and would she care to join him? He was heading towards Asia, and she was welcome to join. So, she said yes. It was her turn to explore the world a little and to travel. The plan was Southeast Asia. She couldn't wait.

Kian and Hayley were so proud of their two children, and in seeing what they were becoming, and how they were developing. They invited them to their family home all the time, and they were always welcome, at the house of Niaina, as they liked to call it. At their artist forest retreat. It was now a real home, and it would be, for generations to come.

Kian and his partner's advertising agency had been bought and integrated into a global one, and Kian had begun to focus more on his photography and his writing. Hayley was lecturing at the College of Psychology. Their love for each other was deep and affectionate; they were not only in love nut also had a sense of respect for each other, and their life paths that constantly intertwined around each other. Together, they had grown and lived their lives, and they were thankful for the family they had created. More than that, they had witnessed the world around them change, and the country rise up and find its power, its voice and its strengths in the greater world, and also stayed humble, cooperative, willing to learn and made space for others. South Africa had turned out pretty damn fine, and so had their lives.

But their lives weren't over yet, and they were determined to make the most of their later retirement too. They had plans to spend some time in Australia and in South America. Their cats, Miss and Martin, were always a concern, but they had found a good house sitter. And so it was that they found themselves on yet another plane, as Hayley liked to say, going 'nowhere', and returning, always to Niaina, which, she said, was 'the place of nowhere', in rough translation.

"If it can be said in ninety minutes, it can be done," was one of the things Kian said time and again. And this, he truly believed. So, he kept writing, his notes turning into memoirs, thoughts, philosophies and ideas for the future. He remembered their long-ago trip to Italy and their visit to the Leonardo da Vinci Museum. He had become a little like this man, with his endless notes, drawings and photographs. This is what his family knew and loved about him. He had a spirit without borders. And so many other things.

The End

Postscript

Kian and Hayley loved each other until the end of their lives. Siena Rose Lina ended up marrying Daniel. They had two children and moved to London. Matt Aslan Luca found love again with a woman named Emma. Together, they had three children. They stayed in Cape Town. Grace also found love. She married a woman called Lola. They adopted a child and moved to New York. Thomas, from San Francisco, stayed in San Francisco. He lived there with his wife, Sandra. The other characters lived happily ever after.